HOLYOKE PUBLIC
250 CHESTNUT
HOLYOKE, MA 01040

DISCARD

D0106090

*Saving Montgomery Sole*

ALSO BY *Mariko Tamaki*

*This One Summer*
*(You) Set Me On Fire*
*Emiko Superstar*
*Skim*
*Fake I.D.*
*True Lies: The Book of Bad Advice*
*Cover Me*

LIBRARY DISCARD

# Saving Montgomery Sole

Mariko Tamaki

SQUARE
FISH

Roaring Brook Press
New York

SQUARE
FISH

An imprint of Macmillan Publishing Group, LLC
175 Fifth Avenue
New York, NY 10010
fiercereads.com

SAVING MONTGOMERY SOLE. Copyright © 2016 by Mariko Tamaki.
All rights reserved. Printed in the United States of America by
LSC Communications, Harrisonburg, Virginia.

Square Fish and the Square Fish logo are trademarks of Macmillan and are
used by Roaring Brook Press under license from Macmillan.

Our books may be purchased in bulk for promotional, educational, or business
use. Please contact your local bookseller or the Macmillan Corporate and
Premium Sales Department at (800) 221-7945 ext. 5442 or by
e-mail at MacmillanSpecialMarkets@macmillan.com.

Library of Congress Cataloging-in-Publication Data

Tamaki, Mariko.
 Saving Montgomery Sole / by Mariko Tamaki.
  pages cm
 Summary: "An outcast teen girl explores the mysteries of friendship, family, faith, and
phenomena, including the greatest mystery of all—herself" — Provided by publisher.
  ISBN 978-1-250-10440-3 (paperback)    ISBN 978-1-62672-272-9 (ebook)
 [1. Self-perception—Fiction.  2. Friendship—Fiction.  3. Clubs—Fiction.  4. Family
life—Fiction.  5. Lesbian mothers—Fiction.  6. California—Fiction.]  I. Title.
 PZ7.T1587Sav 2016
 [Fic]—dc23                                                    2015004007

Originally published in the United States by Roaring Brook Press
First Square Fish Edition: 2017
Book designed by Andrew Arnold
Square Fish logo designed by Filomena Tuosto

3  5  7  9  10  8  6  4  2

LEXILE: 690L

*To DBT,*
*who has saved me many times*

We shall not cease from exploration
And the end of all our exploring
Will be to arrive where we started
*And know the place for the first time.*

—T. S. Eliot

## 1

I USED TO HAVE A T-SHIRT THAT HAD THE WORDS
NEVER STOP EXPLORING on it.

On the front was a starry moonlit sky with puffy text across
the belly. On the back was a tiny ship floating into what I
imagined to be an endless night

When I was in fourth grade, I wore the shirt to show-and-
tell. I said it was my favorite because it had "a moon" on it.

Some kid at the back of the room shouted out, "*The* moon."

"Duh," I said. "There's more than one."

I got a time-out. Because it's not nice to say "duh." Even
though I was right. It *is* "a moon," which I knew back then and
know now. The universe is really big. There's more than just the
one moon that happens to hang over the teeny-tiny town of
Aunty, California, where I live. Have lived. For what feels like
forever.

Although Mama Kate says everything feels like forever when you're sixteen.

*  *  *

It was a crispy but sunny fall afternoon in Aunty. Outside, I could see the shadow of a day moon hanging like an idea in the blue sky. The clock at the front of the clubs room, also Mrs. Dawson's classroom, ticked to 3:31, and I called the meeting of the Jefferson High Mystery Club, Jefferson's smallest student organization, to order.

"Okay," I said, dumping my knapsack on Mrs. Dawson's desk. "Let's do this."

"Right!" Thomas settled his bag on a chair. "Meeting to order!" he boomed. "Members Thomas Masters, Naoki Wood, and *Chair* Montgomery Sole presiding."

"Thank you, Thomas," I said, pulling a cardboard box out of my bag and balancing it on my hand like a tray of drinks. "Thanks for making me a chair."

"Anytime," Thomas said.

"What am I?" Naoki chirped from her perch by the window.

Thomas paused and tapped his chin. "The lamp," he said.

"I love Mondays," Naoki sighed. "Mystery Club is the best."

The official purpose of the Mystery Club, as listed on Jefferson High's hideous garbage-bag-green website, is *Fan Club, Literary*. Which I'm sure is because Mr. Grate, the vice principal, in charge of clubs, teams, and overall student

2

welfare, thinks the Mystery Club is for people who read mystery novels.

The actual purpose of the Mystery Club is to examine unexplained phenomena, curiosities, and other subjects the members consider to be interesting.

Most students at Jefferson High care about things that are the opposite of interesting, such as celebrity weddings, lip gloss, and expensive cars. These things seem interesting, and people obsess about them, but really, if you think of it, stuff like this is not even curious. No one cares about celebrity weddings from twenty years ago. Because they're just ... weddings. A boring person, in lip gloss or a great car, is still boring.

Compare that with black holes, telekinesis, or spontaneous combustion. Spontaneous combustion. No matter when it happened, and to who, it's *always* interesting.

When Thomas and I started the Mystery Club two years ago, before Naoki came to Jefferson, Madison Marlow started a rumor that we were devil worshippers obsessed with aliens.

First of all, kind of a leap between the devil and aliens from outer space.

Second of all, we are neither.

We are examiners of the unknown, Naoki will often say. Voyagers.

Turning, I grabbed a piece of chalk with my free hand and wrote *Remote Viewing* on the chalkboard.

"Remote viewing," I began, swiveling back to the classroom, "is based on the idea that we—all of us—have the ability to see beyond time and space. Yes, Naoki? You don't have to raise your hand."

Naoki dropped her hand into her lap. "I was going to ask, um, could it be possible with this technique to see into the past?"

"Yah," I said. "Like, you know, in ideal circumstances, our mind's eye can see anything, anywhere."

Naoki rubbed her hands together. "I knew this would be good."

"But today we're just focusing on looking into a box," I clarified.

"Cool," Naoki said, waving her hands excitedly. "Sorry to interrupt. Please continue."

"Is this from one of your weird conspiracy theory websites?" Thomas asked, striding to the front of the room and grabbing the cardboard box.

"Yes, it is," I said, snatching it back. "Any *other* questions?"

The stars braided into Naoki's long black-and-white hair twinkled in the sun. "Can I go first?"

"Sure," I said. "Did you bring a mystery item?"

Naoki bobbed her head and twirled toward the front of the room, a lumpy grocery bag in hand. Thomas and I sat down on the floor. Shielding our view with her massive white smock, Naoki tucked her object into the box and tapped the lid closed.

"Okay!" She spun around. "How long does it take to remote view?"

"Give us ninety seconds," I said. I adjusted my overalls, tossed my hair up into a ponytail, and tucked my boots under my knees.

Shifting into a kind of side sit, Thomas flicked a giant dust bunny off the palm of his hand. "And we do this how?" he asked.

"You clear your mind," I said, resting the backs of my hands on my thighs in lotus pose. "We have to open ourselves to our potential."

Thomas ran his hand, flat, in front of his face. "Done!"

"Aaaaand"—Naoki turned and checked the clock—"go."

Remote viewing had been on my list for several weeks as a possible Mystery Club meeting topic. Generally speaking, at every meeting, each member takes a turn presenting a subject they're into. Sometimes we bring in objects or books. Thomas usually shows movies on his laptop, because that's more his thing.

My last presentation was on ESP, during which every two minutes Thomas yelled out, "Oh! I knew that!"

Two weeks ago, Thomas talked about what he deems the great mystery of why Capricorns are really good boyfriends and Aries are not.

At the last meeting, Naoki gave a presentation on lucid dreaming.

When Naoki dreams, she can shape herself and the world around her. She can turn herself into a penguin and swim in the ocean. She can turn herself into a gumdrop or a boot.

Whatever she wants. I've tried this, too, but mostly it just makes me wake up. Thomas says most of his dreams are sexy dreams.

This summer, Naoki had a dream she was a crane, and so, in the real, nondreaming world, she bleached her hair white and added black tips, like wings.

The site I found on remote viewing didn't exactly say how to do it. It just said, "Clear your mind."

Thirty seconds into sitting down, I was getting pretty much nowhere.

*Wait*, my brain whispered. *I think I see a circle.*

"Time!" Naoki cried.

I opened my eyes and the classroom swam into focus.

Naoki danced over to the box. "So this is like ESP, then?"

"Sort of," I said, pulling myself up from the floor with the grace of what Momma Jo has described as a swan with one leg. "Back in the day, it was used for, uh, psychedelic warfare. Soldiers used it to see into bunkers and stuff."

Thomas stood and dusted off his pants. "For what war specifically?"

"The sixties . . ." I said, trying to sound authoritative.

"Ah. Hmmm. Not a lot of wars being won around then," said Thomas, clearly amused. Thomas is the official Mystery Club skeptic, despite also being the person who wants to talk about Capricorns and superheroes the most.

Naoki clapped. "Okay, so Thomas is first. What's in the box?"

"A hair dryer," Thomas announced, throwing his hands up in the air like a marathoner crossing the finish line.

I raised an eyebrow. "Really. A hair dryer. You *saw* a *hair* dryer."

"Yes," Thomas said, dropping his arms and winking at Naoki.

"Interesting." Naoki nodded.

"You do real-ize," I explained, with exaggerated teacher tone, "that typically with this sort of technique, a person gets a *sense* of the thing."

"Well, I'm *incredibly* gifted at the whole mind-clearing technique," Thomas added with equal exaggeration. "So that probably helps . . . *me*. You know."

Naoki giggled.

"Clearly," I said, switching into my best wise, old alien impression, "your sense of sensing objects is stronger than most. Yes."

"It's a gift," Thomas sighed. "It is my gift and . . . my burden. Also, your Yoda is terrible."

Naoki smiled and hugged herself. "Oh you guys! I love this stuff! Like, sensing! Yes! Your faces were so, um . . ." Naoki rubbed her lips together, feeling out the word. "Triangulated with the object in the box. I could totally see your third eyes."

No one else I know enjoys herself as much as Naoki does doing just about everything. She's like one of those cartoon teddy bears that bursts out in a rainbow glow when she's happy, which is often.

"What did *you* see, Monty?" Thomas said, pointing a wiggling finger at me. "Sorry. What did you *sense*?"

I grabbed at the last image that had danced in front of my eyes. "A circle. Like, a charcoal circle."

"So"—Thomas tapped his chin with his index finger—"not a hair dryer is basically what you're saying."

"Ummmm," I mused. "That wasn't my *sense*, no."

"Naoki, would you enlighten us?" Thomas asked.

Naoki popped off the lid and pulled the object out of the box. "It's a sunflower!"

Silence.

Thomas and Naoki looked at each other, then at me. It was a look similar to the one I got when we did the telekinesis flash cards (which didn't work). A look not unlike the one I got when I brought in spoons for us to try to bend with our minds (which also didn't work).

I could practically see the little puffy "uh-oh" clouds floating above their heads.

"You know what?" Naoki tilted her head, tipped the flower horizontally, then upside down. "It does kind of look a little like a hair dryer," she offered. "Oh!" she added, pointing at the bumpy brown center. "And there is a circle! Do you think that's what you saw, Monty?"

Thomas raised an imaginary scorecard and said in his best game show voice, "Remote viewing: survey says?"

I shrugged. As one of the only fans of anything as cool as remote viewers, sometimes I just wish this stuff would actually work . . . better . . . more.

"I'm giving it a 3.5 out of 5," Thomas continued. "Mostly because I'm shocked it wasn't a hair dryer."

"You're a 3.5!" I said, doing my best to keep a straight face but failing.

"You know that's not true," Thomas cooed. He darted over and threw his arms around me in a massive bear hug. "And you know I love your weird experiments even if they never work."

"*Sometimes* they work," I huffed. "It's complicated."

"Well, I love them anyway," Thomas said.

"You love *me*," I said.

"Mostly, yes," Thomas said, giving me a small shove. "Even though you are bossy and made me sit on the floor in my new pants."

"What? I'm not bossy!" I grinned. "I'm the chair!"

"Well," Naoki said, lowering the flower back into the box, "I thought it was pretty cool. Now my turn."

\* \* \*

By the time we'd finished remote viewing all there was to view, or not, since no one "saw" any of the articles we brought, it was almost five thirty.

"Sometimes I feel like we enter a time vortex when we do Mystery Club." Naoki sighed happily as she trotted down the front steps.

"Time flies when you're seeing through walls," Thomas added.

"Have we done vortexes yet?" I asked, grabbing my phone out of my pocket to check.

When we got to the curb, Naoki's dad was there to take her to her pottery class.

Naoki's dad has hair longer than mine, and he wears it in a big bun at the top of his head.

"Let's go!" He waved from the car. "Hi, kids."

"Hi, Mr. Wood," Thomas and I greeted in unison, in that upbeat but drone-like voice you have to use when you're talking to someone's parents.

"Bye." Naoki waved as she hopped into the car.

Thomas had a coffee date.

"Toodle-loo," he said, blowing me a kiss as he ran off.

Because I refuse to take part in any activities beyond the one I sort of created for myself, I had nothing to do. So I went home, comforted by the quiet, the warm breeze that is the autumn air in California, and the sound of my boots hitting the concrete as I marched to the bus.

\* \* \*

I love my house.

It has a massive pine tree in the front yard that looks like we have a magical creature in a big, pointy, feathered hat squatting on the front lawn. Mama Kate is afraid that one day it will fall on the house, and my sister, Tesla, used to have these crazy nightmares from the shadows the branches cast on her wall. But I love it. It smells like rain.

After the obligatory parental hellos and a hastily zapped microwaved burrito (Monday being the one night of the week we are allowed to eat wherever we want), I bolted up to the cozy paradise also known as my room. As soon as I was in, I kicked off my boots; slipped into my supersoft and paper-thin

FRANKIE SAYS RELAX T-shirt and gym shorts; and flopped into the supercomfy armchair I have set up by my desk, which was an old kitchen table so it still smells like onions in some spots.

"Oh, hello, Internet," I cooed as I flipped open the lid to my ancient but fully functional laptop.

I can lose a whole weekend ignoring the natural beauty of the fabulous state of California to read weird stuff online. Last year I spent a month obsessing over this woman who blogs and live-tweets about what she calls her "process of becoming a human cyborg." Later I read an article that said she had to give it up because she was hallucinating, possibly due to lead poisoning from all the bolts and screws she was inserting under her skin.

Which, you know, is a little scary.

After polishing off my burrito, I spent an hour just clicking around the web.

I find most of my Mystery Club topics through random searches, which I keep track of in this app I found that was designed for overachieving businessmen.

There's a happy-face list, originally for listing good habits, where I keep all the mysteries I consider worth looking into:

☺ ESP
☺ That thing that lets people bend spoons

And there's an unhappy-face list, which is technically for tracking bad habits, but I use it, because it's there, for tracking

11

those things I do not understand and never will, and don't care.

☹ Flip-flops
☹ People's obsession with getting rid of all body hair

That night I was hoping to find a better psychic experiment and a more thorough explanation of how a person would actually see something psychically. I typed in a few questions along the lines of, *How can you see something someone else is seeing if you're not in the same place?*

Alternately, I had this idea that I would find something about crystal balls.

I clicked something. Read something. Got a root beer. Came back. Watched a video of kittens playing guitars. Clicked something, and then I clicked something else, and before I knew it, there was a link to this other thing and a link to a website. And presumably, that is how I ended up at:

Manchester's Academy of Magic,
Mystical Forces, and New Believers

Which is weird because I was really not looking for anything specifically mystical, or magic, and I don't remember clicking a link about anything like that.

But suddenly there I was.

The website looked like it was designed in the nineties. The banner was in Times New Roman. Underlined. Top center, framed in lavender, was this drawing of a troll-like two-headed woman in a black cape. Like, the worst picture ever drawn.

Most of the text was about different kinds of mysteries. A lot of it was stuff I'd read before about different legends in different countries: fairy folk in England, the Huldufólk in Iceland. There was something about the Loch Ness Monster, which I'm sure has to appear on every website about anything magical or strange. For a second I thought maybe it was a *Dungeons & Dragons* fan site because there were a few *ye*s and *yore*s in there.

Ye-ancient-powers-of-yore-type stuff.

At some point, I clicked an *About* link next to a wizard picture, because, you know, *About* what? About wizards? Maybe something about spells?

Instead, the link took me to a page that was completely blank, except for a *Store* link.

Where there was only one thing listed.

THE EYE OF KNOW

Next to the title was a picture, like some sort of badly lit cell phone picture, of this white rock laid out on a piece of black velvet.

```
Completely genuine crystal amulet.
Rock excavated from asteroid landing
in the magical mountain ranges of
```

Peru. When wielded by a skilled
visionary, the eye is a portal to
vision untold. Journey forward into
insight. Explore the power of know.
Amulet comes with adjustable leather
strap and may be worn as a necklace,
bracelet, or anklet. Instruction
booklet included. Only $5.99!

When was the last time anyone you knew *wielded* anything?

I thought, *Maybe it's just a piece of rock from some guy's backyard. Possibly in Manchester.*

"'A portal to vision untold,'" I said to no one but the possibly unseen paranormal presences in my room.

What if it was . . . a portal?

Plus it was only $5.99. *That's, like, a cup of coffee and a doughnut,* I thought.

Looking at the site, I paused to suck out the last dregs of my root beer.

Couldn't be any worse than trying to see inside a box.

*Why not?* I thought.

Fortunately, I have a credit card for just such occasions. Which I must, with no exception, pay off every month with my meager allowance or it gets taken away, because my moms are afraid kids today don't have the same appreciation for money that they did "back in the old days." Not that I do that much shopping.

After my purchase, I went downstairs for a snack. My

moms and Tesla, my younger sister, were sitting in the living room, watching TV. I say "my moms" a lot because I think of them as one being from time to time . . . They are two separate people. Momma Jo is tall; Mama Kate is short. Momma Jo is loud; Mama Kate is not.

Momma Jo says stuff like, "You look too un-busy for someone your age. Did you do your homework?"

Mama Kate says stuff like, "Did you want to talk about something?"

I'm told there was a time when I called Momma Jo "Bobo" and Mama Kate "Mama." A little insulting, I'm sure, since Bobo was also the name of my favorite stuffed elephant, a present from Momma Jo for my second birthday.

"Fortunately," Momma Jo often notes, "you grew out of that."

As I slipped past the living room, the moms were getting ready to watch some show about a woman who is happy with her job but sad about her love life.

Tesla was on the carpet, still in her special workout gear, because even though Tesla is only eleven, she does yoga every day. To keep her core lean. Apparently this requires special clothes. "Breathing clothes," Tesla calls them.

I can't watch TV with my moms anymore, because they won't stop asking me stuff.

Every time we sit down to watch TV, they immediately dive into this weirdly pointless Q and A.

"Did you know about this Facebook bullying thing, Montgomery?"

*No.*

"Oh look, Monty! Is that a Goth?"

*Ugh. NO.*

"Gluten-free. Montgomery, isn't that like wheat-free?"

*No clue.*

"Hey, Montgomery, is that the same actor as the one in the movie that you like?"

Sometimes I wonder what would happen if I said, "I have no idea what you're talking about, *moms*, because you haven't included any actual names in that sentence. So let's say *no*."

They'd probably just zoom onto the next question. "What was the name of that play you did last year? Was it *Hamlet*, Montgomery?"

*No, in fact, it was called* I'm trying to watch TV.

It's easier if I just watch stuff by myself, upstairs in my room, on my parental guardian–monitored Netflix account.

As I padded through the hallway, passing the living room on my way to the kitchen, Momma Jo turned and popped her head up over the couch. "Hey! Monty!" she shouted, pointing at the screen. "Didn't we watch something like this before? About this woman but in the other show she was a doctor? Is that possible? Monty! Montgomery! Hello? What are you doing?"

"Nothing," I said, slip-skating across the floor. I was weirdly kind of happy. Like, not laughing-for-no-reason happy, but at least a little happy. Like a kid who's just discovered that socks on hardwood floors is like skates on ice. I twirled a perfect 360 and skidded into the kitchen.

*The Eye of Know*, I thought as I perused the cupboards for the perfect snack. The words felt good swishing around in my brain. *Eye. Know. All.* Possibly my greatest discovery?

"What's up with you?" Mama Kate chirped, stepping into the kitchen, the popcorn bowl dangling empty by her side. "Are you going to watch TV with us?"

"Nothing," I said. "And, uh, I'm doing work upstairs, so not tonight."

"Your clothes are so big and old. You look weird," Tesla huffed as she wandered in behind Mama Kate. "Where's the popcorn?"

"They're supporting my core," I retorted.

"Do you want new clothes?" Mama Kate asked, raising an eyebrow. "I feel like we're overdue for a shop."

"Nah. I'm good."

I'd been doing just fine on Goodwill finds and mom hand-me-downs. Momma Jo didn't mind my duds.

Many of them were her castoffs.

Flinging the freezer door open, I grabbed one of the cartons of fancy blueberry gelato and beat it back up to my room.

Then I texted Thomas.

Me: Date done? Call me.

I guess you could say that Thomas is kind of like my big-brother-slash-best-friend because he's supermature, and I say this not just because he's a year older than I am (and a grade ahead).

I have often told him that, technically, that should make us even, since boys are so much less mature than girls.

Scientifically proven, by the way.

Thomas says gay boys mature faster than straight boys because they pay more attention to the world around them.

That night Thomas came on the phone humming the theme from some cartoon series he's obsessed with.

I said, "Does shopping online ever make you inexplicably happy?"

Thomas considered. "Um, sometimes. What did you buy?"

"A crystal from a really ugly website."

Thomas snorted. "You and Naoki and your crystals and your dreams."

"How was your date?" I said.

"My date with The Butcher?" I could tell he was painting his nails because I was clearly on speakerphone and he was taking little pauses of concentration. "He's an urban poet. An urban poet and . . . a butcher."

"Surprise, surprise."

Thomas says his dating life doesn't define him. It's all just fodder for his creative sensibility, he says. Sometimes it feels like his dates are characters from a movie.

"What happened to the Yoga Master?" I asked.

"Not so masterful."

"Butchers are probably cooler," I added.

"Oh, let me tell you," Thomas cackled, bumping the phone, "the kids in Aunty are all over the butchers. And the butches! These girls think it's quite the thing."

I flipped over on the bed so I could put my face on the pillow, mashing the phone against my ear. I released my ponytail and was blanketed in hair.

"Did you really think the remote viewing was 3.5?" I asked.

"Is 3.5 bad? Maybe on a game show," Thomas said. "I would say I'm not clear on why you would need to remote view anything now that we have smart phones."

"Well," I said, "it would be cool, though. To have that kind of skill in your back pocket. Just in case."

Thomas paused. "Just in case what?"

"I don't know." I rolled onto my back and stared at the chalk spirals Momma Jo had helped Naoki and me draw on my ceiling a few months ago.

"In case we need to start a psychedelic war?" Thomas asked. "Is that what we're doing next week?"

"I'm not planning anything. I'm just saying. It would be cool. To be able to see."

*To actually see*, I thought, *and to know*. Just because remote viewing was a 3.5 didn't mean a 5.0 wasn't out there, somewhere.

I sat up. "I should go," I said. "I haven't even done my English homework yet."

"Good night, Montgomery Sole."

"Good night, Thomas."

I turned on some Echo & the Bunnymen because the guy has this great voice and they have this song "The Killing Moon" that I really like. I grabbed my school copy of *The Outsiders* and flopped back onto my bed.

That night, somewhere, someone, hypothetically, in Manchester, or Pocatello, or even next door, was boxing up my Eye of Know, sealing it in brown paper and tape.

Right before I fell asleep, I pulled out my phone and opened my app.

☺ The Eye of Know

# 2

"MONTGOMERY AND TESLA SOLE! IF YOU ARE NOT IN *the car in six minutes, you are on foot!*"

Ah, the dulcet tones of the Sole household in the morning, the gentle song of the morning Momma Jo.

It was 8:34 a.m., and my house—as it is at 8:34 *every day*—was late for school, and my moms were freaking out. As I pulled myself into my overalls and grabbed a T-shirt from the floor, I could hear my moms running after Tesla, who can never find her socks—*ever*—or her books, or anything, really.

*"There's just a green one here!"* Tesla screamed, running down the stairs.

*"Then put on a green one and another one!"* Momma Jo yelled.

What happens to us between breakfast and 8:34 a.m.? A mystery for the ages.

*"No! Mommmmaaa!"*

Honestly, for someone who can never find them, my sister cares a lot about socks. I can't imagine caring that much about something as ridiculous as *clothes*. Not even clothes—*socks*. Why would anyone care about a piece of clothing that's designed to be on the stinkiest part of your body?

I peered out my bedroom door to see if it was safe to make a break for the stairs.

"Tesla, I found a green one. Come here," Mama Kate called, rushing upstairs, dangling a kneesock like a garter snake from her fingers.

*"I don't want green socks! I need my pink soccer socks!"*

*"Montgomery and Tesla Sole,"* Momma Jo hollered as she stomped out of the kitchen and toward the front door. *"Two minutes!"*

Every once in a while, driving to school—or being driven to school, until I am seventeen—I look at the vast blue sky and the rolling green hills, and I think that there must be some kid living in some industrial town like Detroit or Pittsburgh or something, some town with, like, gray skies and coal for air, who *dreams* of living in a place like Aunty. I bet you this kid wakes up every morning and listens to Vampire Weekend or some other Cali-pop tune and thinks, *Gee, if only I could live somewhere where the sun is always shining, where the sparkling blue ocean caresses the coast . . .*

And so on.

To this kid, I would say, "It's not as great as it sounds."

I mean, first of all, not every town in California is San Francisco or LA.

When I first heard "California," I thought we were moving to Hollywood. Granted, I was nine.

And, honestly, the fact that the sun is always shining here is pretty much an indication that we're all about to die of global warming. I don't think it's anything to get all tra-la-la about, unless your only goal in life is to get an amazing tan and learn how to skateboard.

The only reason to love the sun here is the resulting plentitude of avocado, which is basically my favorite thing in the world to eat. Especially on rye toast. With just a little bit of salt and pepper. And a drop or two of really good olive oil.

According to Momma Jo, who is from Blenheim, Ontario, which is in Canada, which is very cold, there are many places in the world where it is not possible to pick an avocado from your avocado tree in the backyard for breakfast.

Horrific.

That said, I wonder if students in Blenheim, Ontario, have to suffer through a school pep rally every month.

A rally that, by the time I got to school, was in full craziness.

I crawled up into the nosebleed section to join Thomas, a book hidden in my Jefferson High WE'RE #1 foam finger for later.

Sipping from a box of the latest health elixir, Thomas gave me a tiny wave. "Good morning, Montgomery. I hope you are prepared to cheer for the home team."

I stabbed my finger clumsily into the air, almost dropping my book.

The crowd roared.

Thomas yawned and popped an earbud into his left ear.

"Can you imagine the whole school gathering every month to cheer on the Mystery Club?" I asked. "Or anything like it? Like, even the Dramedy Club?"

"Is this the start of a joke?" Thomas asked, slipping his shuffle into his pocket and adjusting his velvet blazer (lined with school colors, or at least Thomas's version of Jefferson High green).

It's a pretty tragic name. *Dramedy.* I don't think there's really any reason to rally around a name like that.

Every time I hear the name, I can picture some teacher desperate for student participation trumpeting, "Hey, you guys, wanna come have fun with theater?"

Thomas is actually a longtime, upstanding member of the Dramedy Club, in part because he wants to be a director someday. When school is making him crazy, he imagines he's making a movie about a wayward high school population.

Sometimes as he's walking to class, he puts his fingers up in a frame and pans across his shots.

Also, he has a tendency, when we're walking down the hall, to lean into me and whisper, *"Action!"*

Naoki is also originally from Canada, from Vancouver, where there are no pep rallies to be had. I remember the first rally she went to, the year before. She was like a kid going to Disneyland.

"A pep rally? And everyone goes," she'd marveled, "to raise *spirit* for the school? Wow. Do they sing?"

"They shout," Thomas had said.

"It's more of a scream," I'd added, jumping and swinging my arms. "It's like this: '*Ahhhhhhhh, Jefferson High, aaaaaahhhhhhh-hhh!*'"

"Wouldn't it be great if we *sang*?" Naoki had said. "That would be so amazing!"

That day, as Thomas and I sat and chatted, and Thomas half listened to dance music, Naoki swayed and twirled around the top row with two foam fingers (one was Thomas's) pointed at the ceiling. She looked like a cloud with a foam finger wedged on either side.

Probably the first thing I noticed about Naoki was that she always wears white. Not like tennis white, or yuppie white, but what Thomas calls hippie white—long, flowing skirts and shawls. White like lilies and like smoke. She paints her nails white and sometimes she paints white spirals on her cheeks. And even though it's not weather appropriate, sometimes she wears a baby-blue knitted scarf because she says her neck misses scarves.

It seems a little underplayed to say that something about Naoki is weirdly, like, magical.

I'm pretty sure she basically just *is* magic.

Most of the people at this school think that Naoki's a space cadet. Partly because she has this way of answering questions that's kind of long and meandering, and people are always cutting her off and rolling their eyes. I'm pretty sure she doesn't care, though, or at least I've never seen her get mad.

I long ago added the pep rallies to my list of things I do not care to understand:

- ☹ Stupid pep rallies—which everyone else seems to love for no reason
- ☹ Why the lyrics to our cheer are called lyrics even though it's just *Jefferson High!*

Although I do think it would be cool to study something that actually raises spirits.

☺ Chanting?

\* \* \*

After the rally, I had math, which is never fun. Mr. Deever is the sweatiest person on the planet. One day he's just going to melt into a puddle in front of us like that guy in *X-Men*.

Second period. English.

As soon as I sat down, Mrs. Farley announced we were doing group work, which meant I had to spend the whole period with Madison Marlow and the Parte twins, Cat and Miffy. Who *immediately*, upon hearing my name lumped with theirs, rolled their eyes and shook their platinum-blond ponytails in unison. I combed my hair over my face.

*Great.*

"Oh my God," I heard Madison whisper. "Is she wearing farmer pants?"

I looked down. My overalls were looking a little worn-more-than-once. Not that that was any of Madison's business.

"They go with her Def Leppard T-shirt," Cat snickered.

*Def Leppard?* I looked down.

*It's Death Cab for Cutie, idiots,* I wanted to scream. Not exactly the same thing. Of course, it's hard to scream something at someone when you're in the process of scooting your desk over to join her group.

Since fourth grade, Madison Marlow and the Parte twins have basically been the heads of the Aunty blond mafia. Madison's mom runs just about every group (gardening, bridge, ladies' softball, scrapbooking, felting, knitting, ladies' chess, and Pilates) in Aunty. So Madison had no choice, clearly, but to be the same way and run everything at Jefferson, a dictator in short shorts and too much mascara.

It tells you something about the student population, I think, that they've surrendered power to someone who once said, out loud, that girls who don't wear bras are prone to depression.

Mrs. Farley asked us to look up examples of irony and foreshadowing in *The Outsiders*.

We didn't even get to irony.

Four minutes in, Madison took charge.

"We have to look for dark things," she said, flipping through her book, using her ridiculous fake nails like tiny spatulas.

*Dig. Flip. Dig. Flip.*

"Right! It's totally night at the beginning of the book, I think," Miffy offered.

"Wait," I cut in, turning to Miffy. "What's that got to do with foreshadowing?"

My assigned group threw ice-cold girl glares.

"Foreshadowing has nothing to do with night," I explained—I thought, hopefully.

Silence.

"It *doesn't*," I said.

"Um, I didn't say it did," Madison hissed, waving her nails so close to my face I could smell the epoxy. "We're looking at, like, dark things that show that things are going to get . . . bad. And, um, guess what. As Miffy knows, night is dark."

"God, Montgomery," Miffy huffed, rocking back in her seat and flicking her ponytail over her shoulder like a weapon.

I squirmed in my desk, my student-issued classroom torture device. Cat coiled the end of her ponytail around her index finger.

"Foreshadowing doesn't have to be dark," I said finally. It felt like I was squeezing the words out of my eyeballs.

"Hey," Madison snapped. "There's no need to be rude!"

"I'm not being rude. I'm being right!" I could feel my cheeks glowing red. I'm sure I was flushing like crazy. I probably looked like a raspberry.

"Excuse me. Can I just say? A shadow is *dark*." Cat sniffed, looking at Madison.

"That's totally true." Madison nodded.

"Uh, *hello*, I know that," I said, my face exploding. "What I'm saying is, that doesn't mean foreshadowing has to be dark!"

*Honestly!*

Mrs. Farley stopped writing on the blackboard and looked over at our group. Someone else on the other side of the classroom coughed. *"Whi-itch."*

"Whatever," Madison sneered. "Let's just work without her."

And they scooted their chairs closer together and bent their heads toward each other so I could just hear them whispering. *"It's like, 'Oh, I'm so cool, look at my T-shirt, I listen to alternative music.'"*

I could feel my stomach pinching together like someone was using it to make pizza.

As a kid, I thought girls being mean was the only way to get a stomachache.

Screw them. I inched my chair over in the other direction and held my book in my lap so I could be as far away from them as the class rules of "group work" allowed.

"Does anyone have any examples?" Mrs. Farley asked, pacing up the aisle. "Anyone? No? Not even one? Nice work, guys. Okay, it's homework, then."

The bell rang.

"Class dismissed," Mrs. Farley sighed.

Just to make sure I really got that feeling-like-a-busted-up-sandbox-toy vibe, after lunch, I ran into Matt Truit.

Matt is one of the most popular boys at Aunty, even though he just transferred here last year. He is the biggest jock there is, the best football and basketball player of all time, irresistible to all women. Also, he is a jerk.

So Thomas and I were walking down the hall to class, talking about whether or not it would be cool to go to Disneyland for my birthday, which is maybe out of the question because we'd probably have to rent a hotel room since it's really far. Thomas thought we should try to hitch to Vegas or something. Which is probably also out of the question but still fun to talk about hypothetically. And we bumped into Matt. Or Thomas did. And Matt spun around and said, "I thought you gays, I mean, guys, were supposed to be light on your feet."

Thomas and I kind of simultaneously froze midstep.

And Matt smiled. This stupid, big, puffy lip smile. This smile like an old pizza crust. And he said, "*Joke.*"

I felt Thomas's hand on my back, and we started walking again.

"Jerk," I whispered.

"I know, I know." Thomas breezed past the lockers, head held high. "Let's go, Monty, heel, toe, heel, toe, nice strut. This is the scene where we march off into our futures. Cue bell."

And right on cue, the school bell screamed. *BRRRRRRING!*

Thomas ran off to gym. I ran to bio, just in time to find out that I'd failed my test because I drew a plant cell instead of an animal cell.

"Seriously?" I groaned to myself.

Clearly displeased with our overall cell ignorance, Mr. Jenner took a swig from his massive coffee thermos and said, "Okay, let's go through our answers. Eyes front. Mr. Tanner, I'm talking to you. *Mr. Tanner, this class is not a party for you to meet girls!*"

In history, Mrs. Dawson had the flu, so we watched some ancient DVD of a BBC production of *King Lear*. What that has to do with ancient China, which is what we're studying, I'm not sure.

Then I was supposed to have study hall, but I kind of wandered the halls for a bit, feeling a little lost, until I ran across Naoki heading into the library for her English class.

I told her what had happened with Thomas and Matt. She frowned. "Poor Thomas," she said.

"Matt is, like, 'Oh I'm so funny,'" I spat. "Like that guy even knows what a joke is. That guy is as funny as . . ."

"A rock?" Naoki offered.

"That would be an insult to rocks," I said, thinking of the cool white surface of the Eye of Know.

"Rocks *are* pretty great." Naoki paused, tracing something in the palm of her hand. "It's too bad Matt isn't the person you thought."

Which is Naoki's nice way of saying, or remembering, that I once had kind of a thing with Matt Truit. *Briefly* had a thing with Matt Truit.

"There should be an actual foreshadowing technique that lets you avoid this stuff," I said.

"Maybe there is." Naoki patted my shoulder with her scarf. "Healing scarf touch," she explained.

"Uh, thanks."

Naoki smiled encouragingly. Which made me think maybe

I was looking like a basket case. Which I am not. I straightened, crossed my arms over my chest in order to look casual and in control.

"Hey," I said. "Did I tell you I ordered this thing on the Internet yesterday? The Eye of Know. We're going to wield it and use it to see beyond."

The word *wield* clearly peaked Naoki's interest. "We're going to wield the Eye of Gnome! That's fabulous!"

"The Eye of *Know*," I said. "*Know*, like with a *k*. Like *knowledge*."

"Oh," Naoki breathed. "Oh, I haven't heard of that one."

"But you've heard of an Eye of *Gnome*?"

I must have said it really loudly. There was a shuffling inside the library. "Naoki," a soft librarian voice called, "please take your seat."

"Crap," I said, stepping back. "I should go."

"Do you want to go walk in the sun later?" Naoki asked, stepping one toe through the library door. "We can talk about the Eyes?"

"No, it's okay," I called, walking backward down the hallway. "See you later."

Slumped over in study hall, I realized the only thing that could save me on a day like this was frozen yogurt.

# 3

BEFORE YOGGY WAS YOGGY, IT WAS THIS ANTIQUE
shop owned by a woman who always wore pink tracksuits
and told her customers that the place was haunted. Mama
Kate went there all the time because she likes old things like
candlesticks and lace doilies. While she shopped, I sat at the
front and grilled the woman about the ghost.

It used to make me crazy that she couldn't be more specific.

"What's her name?" I would ask.

"I don't know, dear," she'd say, needlessly dusting the very
old things in the shop.

"But it's a girl?" I'd push, watching the dust spray up and
land back on the glass or wood she was cleaning.

"It's a feminine spirit."

I considered this. "When she talks, can you hear it in your
brain or your ear?"

"You buying anything, little girl? Or just riling up an old woman for kicks?"

Clearly this was just laziness on the old lady's part because I can go online and in two seconds find, like, intensive documentation people have done all over the world of the different paranormal spirits inhabiting their houses and other buildings. I could go online right now and buy a Spirit Tracker if I was so inclined. There's a guy in Iowa who sells them for, like, a hundred bucks (plus shipping). Last year I found this one site where this guy had a twenty-four-hour webcam of his haunted closet (although I watched for about three hours nonstop once, and I didn't see anything).

Whoever bought the place and put up Yoggy clearly repurposed some of the art and decor from the antique shop. The place is covered in a mishmash of old posters from the fifties to the nineties. Thomas, when he's accompanied me to get a treat, says the place feels a little sacrilegious.

"You mean, like, haunted?"

"Ugly, Monty. *Ug-ly.*"

Tiffany, who is both the manager and the only person who works at Yoggy, is sort of my adult best friend. She looks kind of more like a mountain lion than a person. She has big dreads, which I normally don't like on not–African American people, but on Tiffany it looks kind of scary in a good way. She's got all these thick black tattoos on her forearms. On one hand is a hammer and on the other is a fountain pen. On her back is a picture of a woman holding a sign that says "No justice, no peace." Tiffany wears tank tops even though it's always freezing at Yoggy. Tiffany used to be a master's student in Women's Studies in Michigan, but then she said she decided the whole thing was useless and too expensive. Also, her boyfriend ran off to India with a skinny yoga instructor . . . named Tiffany.

What are the odds?

Now Tiffany spends most of her time at Yoggy working on her "independent thesis," which will be based on her "out-of-system" research on "The SorBetties."

The SorBetties are the yoga freaks who come to Yoggy every week but only ever eat the health-conscious options, that is, the yogurt Yoggy has labeled as either fat- or sugar-free. Or carb-free. Tiffany has been tracking the SorBetties' movements since she got this job three years ago. Every time a SorBetty orders a health-conscious Yoggy flavor, Tiffany takes their picture with her phone and adds them to her data.

We got to be friends because one day I ordered health-conscious, carb-free, blueberry swirly with extra marshmallow and Cocoa Puffs topping, and I caught her taking my picture. My only interest in the carb-free blueberry was that it was their only blueberry option. Blueberry goes great with marshmallow.

I would never diet. Even Tesla, who is always on a health kick, would never diet. You cannot diet in a house run by lesbian moms, especially when one of them was the head of a "consciousness-raising group" in college.

Or, you know, that's what Momma Jo tells me.

Needless to say, Tiffany and I are pretty much bonded on

our shared major dislike for the population of Aunty that worries about carbs. The SorBetties are *the* rudest. They always travel in packs and squeal really loudly like how girlfriends laugh on TV. Also, they never pick up their cartons. And they never finish their yogurt.

Recently, Tiffany kicked her research up a notch by changing around the health-conscious cards on some of the flavors. The Wild Strawberry Sensation, as a result, is now listed as carb-free.

It is not.

It's possible the SorBetties have sensed a snake in the grass.

"This is *totally* carb-free?" they squeak from the dispensers. "You're sure? Totally carb-free? Hellooooo, yogurt lady? I'm talking to you. Yes. Are you *absolutely* and *totally sure* this is carb-free?"

"Totally." Tiffany has a special smile she saves for the SorBetties. It is a teeth-only, dead-eye smile. It looks like some sort of reverse magic spell.

Mystery Club–related side note: once, like two years ago, I started reading these blogs of girls who decided to starve themselves to death. I was actually looking for websites about people who fast for spiritual reasons, so they can hallucinate, but all these anorexia fan sites started coming up instead.

There are so many blogs out there written by girls who want to weigh less than a baby squirrel.

I would put it on my list of things I will never understand, but it's too gross and sad.

Of course, the second-best part of Yoggy is that whenever I come in, Tiffany lets me put on as much topping as I want as long as I pay for the actual yogurt.

I'm currently perfecting the perfect balance of mochi and mandarin slices and crispy stars. The trick is to keep the stars on the top so they don't get soggy.

The store was quiet when I arrived, so Tiffany let me sit on the counter, and we looked at sexist magazines together. Which was kind of calming. The counters were all littered with half-eaten cups of strawberry-smelling goop.

"How's the research?" I asked, between perfect cold and crunchy mouthfuls.

"Grueling," Tiffany grumbled.

I scooped some extra Lucky Charms cereal and maraschino cherries on my Mocha Me Crazy fro even though Mama Kate is convinced anything with red dye is poison.

Flipping the page of her magazine, Tiffany squished her mouth from side to side, like she was rinsing with Listerine or something. Her lip ring looked a little sore.

"How's school?" she asked.

"Stupid," I said, flipping the magazine page.

"Huh." Tiffany flashed a pierced-eyebrow raise.

"Hey," I said, jumping off the counter to grab more topping. "Do you ever get the feeling you're, like, on the verge of not being able to deal with people being jerks?"

Tiffany gave me the look I guess a person like me asking a person like her a question like that deserves. I mean, she works at a place called Yoggy.

She sighed and grabbed another magazine from the pile. "High school is mostly pointless."

"Right." I stabbed at a handful of peanut butter cups with my clearly-too-small-for-the-job set of plastic tongs. "I'm pretty convinced my own research online will be more fruitful than anything I'll learn at Jefferson High."

Tiffany stopped to unstick a page. The magazines were the ones the SorBetties had left behind, and they were always covered in carb-free. "Yep. Most of what you're learning at school is a lie you'll have to unlearn in college."

"Unlearn!" I shouted exuberantly, scattering peanut butter cups and cherries on the counter as a result. "Whoops. I mean, exactly! I should just not go."

"Ah, no. You gotta go," Tiffany said, grabbing a wet cloth from under the counter and handing it to me. "Wipe."

"What?" I froze, cloth in hand. "Why?"

"Ahem. You gonna clean that up?"

Tiffany has this thing, the ability to switch almost who she is, on a dime. Like, all friendly to superharsh. She's not mean like high-school-girl mean. More like grumpy. Usually when something is spilled.

I wiped the counter while she opened up a new magazine.

"You know," she said, when I'd finished grabbing all my spilled toppings with the cloth and dumped them in the trash, "I had a SorBetty come in today and buy a small carb-free for her four-year-old. Four years old, Montgomery!"

I snorted. "What does that have to do with me not going to school?"

Tiffany gave me this kind of drop-dead look. "Maybe there are some things that are bigger than just your problems?"

*Wow. Nice.*

I looked down at what was left in my cup. All I could smell was the bleachy, sour smell of the wet rag on my hands. The anti-food smell.

*You know, I wanted to say, I'm, like, the only person you talk to all day, I bet, that gets why it sucks here. I mean, it's not like I treat you like someone who's serving me yogurt. How about you treat me like something other than a dumb kid?*

Instead I said, "Well, thanks for the toppings."

Just then, the door dinged and a bunch of SorBetties came in, dewy from Ashtanga or whatever it is they do. I slipped out, put a little Eurythmics on. Eurythmics is this band from the eighties. Their song "Here Comes the Rain Again" was Momma Jo's favorite song, and she used to play it *all the time.* I heard it probably a million times as a kid. Fortunately it's a great song. They're probably my fourth-favorite band.

Naoki said it's interesting that I like Eurythmics because the name actually means "a harmonious body of words." "Like a pep rally where everyone is singing the same song."

"And it's a nice song," Thomas added.

☺ Harmony—music and magic?
☺ Throat singing?

There's no way Jefferson High would ever play Eurythmics, anywhere. First of all, Eurythmics is music for poets, not jocks.

39

Plus it's music for singing alone when you feel alone in the world. And that's not pep rally music.

* * *

It was Sole Family Pizza Night. By the time I got home, Tesla had already voted on a movie, *Home Alone*, which is this relatively ancient movie she found on Netflix about this kid who gets left behind when his parents go away, because his parents are stupid and don't know how to count their kids.

As I carefully stacked what I perceived to be the max number of pizza slices onto my plate (accessing my math skills to see if my triangle studies would prove at all helpful—they didn't), I caught Mama Kate looking at me.

"How's it going?" she said, in this superlight "I'm just asking about the weather" way.

"Starving," I said, pointing at my pizza.

Mama Kate disappeared into the fridge and emerged with a big bottle of soda, which is an only-movie-night treat because sugar in pop form makes Tesla a bit crazy. "How's school?"

"Fine," I said. It is important, when eating pizza, to make sure you have at least two napkins per slice. Especially in my family. Half the clothes any of us owns are stained with something.

Mama Kate nudged a glass in my direction. "Nothing of note?"

There is nothing Mama Kate wants more than for me to "talk about things," whatever that means. Talk about what and why is what I want to know. About how Matt Truit is a dickhead? Which would give her a new thing that she can worry about? On top of all the other things she worries about, like food dye and grades and everything? I don't think so.

I poured myself a glass of sugary carbonated goodness and smiled a huge "school photo" fake smile. "Everything's totally cool," I said.

"*Hey!*" Momma Jo shouted from the couch. *"Are we watchin' a movie or what?"*

On movie nights, my moms sit on the couch with Tesla snuggled in the middle, and I perch on the top of the couch, creating kind of a pyramid shape. We have many family photos with this similar formation. It is not necessarily the best setup for a movie-night seating arrangement. Many pieces of pizza have been spilled because the top of the couch, as Momma Jo has often said, is not a table.

I lay a few extra napkins on my knees and on the couch for good measure.

"That's a good idea," Momma Jo said, holding out her hand. "Gimme some of those."

"I might have to go and do homework and not watch the whole movie," I warned as Tesla pointed the remote at the TV.

"Geez. Glad you could join us!" Momma Jo frowned. "How's the pizza? To your liking? Should we order you an extra pie next time?"

"Can I just eat please and not get hassled?" I said, in what was probably more of a low grumble.

"*Hey!*" Momma Jo snapped, flicking my knee. "How about

you're wearing my super cool overalls so you should be nice to me or I'll let Mama take you shopping for real clothes?"

"Jo, stop it!" Mama Kate reached up and patted my leg. "I'm glad you're still into movie night," she whispered.

"*Shhhh!*" Tesla pouted. "I'm trying to watch."

Tesla was superintense through the whole movie. At some point she slid off the couch and sat cross-legged on the floor, so she could practically touch the TV. Against the screen, her hair looked like a halo.

At some point, the kid, who has been left alone, goes to a church, because he's lonely, I guess. Tesla made us pause the movie at that scene.

"Why don't we go to church?" she asked.

"Do you want to go?" Momma Jo asked, her mouth full of pizza.

Tesla shrugged and pressed Play.

Mama Kate looked hard at the back of Tesla's head.

*Weird.*

But then, of course, before I could think about it too much, true to form . . .

"Oh! It's that woman! What's the name of that actress, Monty?"

*I have no idea.*

"You know this little boy is grown up and married now, I think. Isn't he, Monty?"

*For God's sake.*

Right about the time the zany burglars in the movie were

slipping around on marbles, which Momma Jo thought was hilarious, I began my escape.

"You don't want to see the end of this?" Momma Jo asked as I slid backward off the couch, not unlike a lizard.

"I think I got it," I said, landing on the floor and standing upright. "The kid ends up not alone, right?"

"*Monty!*" Tesla whined.

"Sorry!" I hollered, and bounded up the stairs.

* * *

I was lying in bed when I got an IM from Thomas.

> Thomas: You OK? Looked for you after school.
> Me: Bad day. Jefferson sucks.
> Thomas: Cour-age, my little one.
> Thomas: Remember we are orchids in a forest of carnations.
> Me: I will try.

I think the thing that really makes Thomas, me, and Naoki such good friends, beyond their amazingness, is the fact that we are most definitely—unlike everyone else in Aunty—not from here.

Technically, I've lived here since I was nine. But let's just say, as a girl with two moms, from Canada, I didn't exactly get a warm welcome when I stepped through the doors of Aunty Public Elementary School, vintage Michael Jackson lunch box in tow.

And the number of times, since that first day, that I've been asked if I grew up in an igloo is uncountable.

I've also been asked, more than a million times, if I miss my dad. By which they presumably mean the anonymous sperm donor who I've never met.

Basically, for as long as I've lived in Aunty, I've always been, like, this inexplicable thing, a mystery object that's not like anyone else at this school. I guess it's possible that that's part of why I'm so obsessed with other inexplicable things. With other unsolved mysteries.

There's nothing wrong with being unsolved. Unsolved just means not everyone gets it.

I'm kind of glad no one else but the Mystery Club is into this kind of stuff. It's like my secret treasure. Me and the Mystery Club's thing. It's special.

After I got off IMing with Thomas, I watched this BBC documentary on cryonics, which is where people freeze themselves so they can be brought back to life in the future. Then I spent a few hours rereading *The Outsiders*.

It's a great book.

I looked up foreshadowing, which—surprise, surprise—doesn't have anything to do with darkness. It's a hint of what's to come that a writer leaves for the reader.

*Why would foreshadowing have to be bad?* I thought. Everything has a shadow. Plus anyone with a brain knows you need a light to have a shadow. Light is good.

I pulled out my phone and opened my app.

☺ Foreshadowing in real life. Maybe fortune telling?

Right under that was:

☺ The Eye of Know

I tossed my phone on the bed and looked up the website, just for kicks.

The site was still there, but the shop now had a banner that read *SOLD OUT*.

I called Thomas immediately. "It's sold out!" I cried. "I just checked the website, and the Eye of Know is sold out!"

"Yippee," Thomas yawned.

"Do you think they only had one in stock? Or do you think there are Eyes of Know everywhere?"

"I don't know," Thomas said. "I'll tell you, though, I'm so excited for you to get this stone. I'm thinking, maybe then you won't call me at . . . *midnight*, because you'll *know* that I'm asleep!"

Then he hung up.

And I went to bed, still feeling pretty thrilled.

The Eye of Know.

Was coming.

# 4

☺ Séances
☺ Tea leaf readings
☺ Ouija

PEOPLE WHO WRITE ABOUT OUIJA ON THE WEB HAVE
the spookiest websites. One time I accidentally left one open,
and halfway through the night I could have sworn I heard
whispering coming from my computer, which, needless to say,
meant I spent the night sleeping in my moms' room, curled
up on the floor.

The general consensus among communicating-with-the-
dead experts seems to be that Ouija is a kind of remedial way
to talk to spirits. This one site I found said that the best thing
about Ouija is its clarity. So there's all this chatter, this guy
said, made up of all the souls of the universe, and the Ouija

reaches out into the void and pulls out a single sound, *yes* or *no.*

I don't have that many dead people in my life that I've known, well, except for Momma Jo's parents, who I never met but I've seen pictures of, mostly on vacation in places like Florida and Mexico. In most of the pictures, they are on the beach, fully clothed. Like, shoes and everything.

"That's how old people vacation," Momma Jo had said.

This one time, I found an online Ouija board, where you could put your mouse in the center of the screen and ask a question.

*Call to your spirit,* the site had read. *If the spirit is there, he/she will answer.*

So I asked if Momma Jo's parents were there.

NO.

Then I asked if my biological sperm donor was there. Because I have had this thought, from time to time, that maybe he's dead and maybe he's alive. And it's weird sometimes not to know . . . if he is or not.

"Is my biological sperm donor there—I mean, dead?" I whispered.

NO.

I feel a little guilty whenever I think about or talk about my bio sperm donor. There was a time when I was little, like eight or something, when I was always asking my moms about it, about what I'd called "the stuff" (i.e., sperm).

I'd wanted to know what it looked like.

"What *what* looked like?" Momma Jo asked. I think on that occasion we were waiting in line at the grocery store. "What stuff?"

"*The man sperm!*" I yelled, frustrated.

"*Ha!* Well. Geez. You're asking the wrong person." Momma Jo smirked.

It's not like I want to find him. The donor. I don't need to find him. He's just there, I guess, and sometimes I step on him in my brain, kind of. Like a sock left on the floor.

I don't know if the Ouija thing could be taken as proof that he is alive. I guess it would depend on whether the spirits know what a biological sperm donor is.

No one in Aunty has a clue.

There are some people who consult various forms of spirit communication as a way of preparing for the day. There are apps that will show you your tarot reading every day, presumably so you can decide whether to take the bus or just stay home.

It might be nice to know what's coming your way.

To have an app or an Eye you could touch and say, "Trouble?"

And it would say, "Yes! Avoid the letter *L* at all costs. Also the letter *K* and anything white. And watch out for short men with facial hair."

Or just, "Yes! Go back to bed. Do not pass GO. Do not leave your room until you receive further instruction."

* * *

☺ Morning Music Medleys
☺ Backmasking

If there is one thing the entire student population of Jefferson High, Mystery Club included, can agree on, it is about the Morning Music Medleys. They are just about the worst thing in the world. Imagine if someone took the ugliest parts of every song ever written, in all of time, and mushed them together into one terrible song.

Whoever decided that song should be played in the hallway every day, top volume, from 8:55 a.m. to 8:59 a.m., is not a nice person.

The rumor at school is that this is a punishment, although the official word is it's an effective way to get students to class on time.

I think whoever wrote this so-called medley must look like some sort of cartoon villain. I bet he sleeps on a bed of nails. Naked.

That said, when they started playing the medleys two years ago, the number of kids left in the hallways after bell dropped from tons to, like, four.

This morning, instead of fleeing, I was standing in the hallway so I could record the medley on my phone as part of an independent experiment I was doing on backmasking. Back-masking is this thing where musicians put weird messages in their music, which can only be heard when you play the tracks backward.

Mostly it's just jokes or nonsensical things, like "Who's eaten all the spaghetti?" According to Wikipedia, the rock band Pink Floyd used, "Congratulations. You've just discovered the secret message!"

Of course, all this was back when people had vinyl records and enough time on their hands to play records backward. Which is probably what I would do if I had a record player.

I had this idea one night that maybe there was some sort of messaging in the Jefferson High medley. Something brain-washing like, "Be true to your stupid football team."

Mostly what I was discovering was how much music can penetrate earplugs. Kind of makes you wonder if they're really plugging anything. $5.99 down the drain.

As the music swirled around me, like an angry mob, I stepped up to my locker in a funnel of muffled noise and looked up to see . . . a cross.

When I say "cross," of course I mean a Christian cross, not an *X* marks the spot, although it was probably a little of both. It was white plastic, wallet-sized. Jesus pressed to the front like he was part of the cross instead of nailed to it, his body fused to the slats, his face all contorted and hard to read.

I dropped my bag, suddenly stuck by the cold wave every queer-related kid gets when they see something stuck to their locker that they didn't put there.

See also: KICK ME stickers, MONTYZ MOMZ HAVE AIDS signs, MONTY IS A LESBIAN Post-it notes. You name it. I've had it. It hits, in the same soft spot, right under the lung, every time.

Students dumped their books into bags, slapped lockers closed, scrambled to get out of the hallway.

I felt a tear in the corner of my eye and squeezed it back.

"*No* way. No way. No way. Stop, stop, stop," I whispered. "Stop, stop, stop."

I yanked at the edges of the cross with the tips of my fingers, but it was stuck there. Not even taped. Like, cemented.

Suddenly there was a hard tap on my shoulder. "*Wha wha wha!*"

I jumped and turned to see Mr. Grate, VP, his mouth flapping open and shut like a crazed puppet.

"*Wha wha wha!*"

"What?!" I popped out the earplugs, only to be flooded with noise.

Mr. Grate's face turned red like an overripe tomato. "Class, Miss Sole. Now!"

"Mr. Grate! There's . . ." My face exploding. My fingertips sweaty as they pressed into the hard plastic edge of the newest intruder on my sanity.

"I know, I know. The crosses. We're dealing with it, Miss Sole. There's no need to—"

"I-I don't want it on there!"

"Miss Sole." Mr. Grate leaned so far forward I could practically count his hair plugs. I could definitely smell the cologne he was soaked in. "Our administration will deal with this matter swiftly. In the meantime, you have class. Go. Now."

Looking down the hallway, I saw it. Rows of crosses. Not on every locker, but almost.

"Not the end of the world," Mr. Grate grumbled as he turned and plodded down the hallway, barking out orders. "You! Maxwell! Get to class! You too. Class! Denton! Class! Taft!"

*Who made you the authority on the end of the world?* I seethed.

*No big deal?*

I pressed my lips closed and slammed my locker so hard it made my fingers ring. I snatched my bag and trudged down the hall, awash in a noise that lingered in my brain all through math and Mr. Deever, who despite continued ridiculous sweating, wore a turtleneck to class.

By the time I got to second-period English, my head was throbbing with a magical evil headache. Mr. Gyle, Dramedy Club head, stood at the front of the class with a big yellow sign-up sheet and an unnatural happy grin on his face. Mrs. Farley motioned me to my seat and clapped her hands.

I slid into my chair.

"Okay, class, well today. Yes. Yes, Mr. Totter, sit *down*, please. Yes, so today we have a special announcement and a special guest. This year, Jefferson High will be presenting a full production of *The Outsiders*! Isn't that fun? And Mr. Gyle has agreed to come to class to tell us a little more. Isn't that exciting, class?"

Silence. A sure sign that something is *not* going to be

exciting is when a teacher starts talking about something like it's exciting.

Besides, audition lists had been up in the hallways for weeks. It wasn't exactly *news*.

"Thank you, uh, Mrs. Farley. So. Yes. It's a very tough play," Mr. Gyle explained. "I know you're reading the book, so you know, um, that, well, it's a play with a lot of good themes. But it's not, uh, just literature. Uh, there are fights, and stabbings, so it's a-uh action-type of play. These greasers, these boys, as I'm sure you're noticing in your studies with Mrs. Farley, they were very tough boys, uh guys, and, uh, you know they were the jocks of their time. The, uh, heroes. As it were."

The herd sat lifeless.

"Will there be actual fights onstage?" this kid Todd, amateur rapper and some sort of sport player, asked.

"Oh, uh, yes! Yes, there will definitely be . . . fights. We will be, uh, choreographing, uh, that is to say, uh, *staging* fights."

"Fiiiight," someone whispered in the back of the classroom.

"Looks like Tanner's going to get his butt kicked," someone else chuckled.

"Kick your butt first." Tanner, who I believe is also on a sports team, because he dresses that way, high-fived the kid next to him.

"Kick all your butts," someone else laughed.

"Sign up. We'll see," Tanner barked.

"Okay, enough! Class." Mrs. Farley clapped her hands. "That's enough butts for today."

*Looks like it's butt-kicking time*, I thought. *How thrilling for us all.*

Just to be clear, *The Outsiders* is a book by S. E. Hinton about this kid named Ponyboy, who has a great name but is also really poor. He's what is called a Greaser, which is what the really poor kids from the town he's from are called. And the whole book is about this ongoing battle between the Greasers and the Socs, who are the really rich kids. And the really rich kids beat up and make the Greasers' lives miserable because they can and because they're rich and they get to do whatever they want.

There is no way in hell that the Greasers in *The Outsiders*, by any literary interpretation, are "jocks."

I stared wide-eyed at Mrs. Farley. Like, really? Really, this is happening?

By lunch, the sign-up sheet was a list of almost every jock at Jefferson.

Thomas wanted to eat lunch on the stage in the auditorium, which he has a key to because Mr. Gyle gave him the key two years ago, then forgot to ask for it back. The stage was covered in little taped out X's for where the set would go.

Thomas perched himself on the throne from the *Knights of the Round Table* set, and I sat on an old toadstool from the production of *Alice Through the Looking Glass* many moons ago, balancing my cafeteria fries on my knee. "Did you *know* that Mr. Gyle was going around telling all the jocks they should sign up because it's going to be like Jock Fight Club?"

"*The Outsiders is* about conflict," Thomas sighed, leaning back into his throne and sipping pomegranate juice. "A huge part of the book is fights. Besides, it's an almost all-male cast, and no one was signing up."

"And you care because?" I asked, stabbing my fry into a mound of tangy red goop.

"Because I am a patron of the arts, Montgomery, and I'm on set and wardrobe. And art is art. Art *transcends*."

"Half of these guys can't even read," I grumbled.

Pulling a bag of kale chips out of his pocket, Thomas shrugged. "Well, we're cutting most of their lines for time anyway. It's not worth getting upset about."

"I'm not upset," I said, picking at my toadstool.

"So"—Thomas rolled up his sleeves—"new topic because I don't want to argue about this anymore. Ready? Did you hear about the new student?"

"What new student?"

"Kenneth . . ." Thomas paused. Waited for me to finish chewing my fry, possibly for dramatic effect, possibly because he wanted to let me know I was chewing too loudly. "White."

I paused, mostly because Thomas had just paused, and I wanted to make fun of him a little. "Should that mean something to me?"

Thomas leaned in, eyes wide. "Reverend White? Reverend John White? Reverend 'I'm going to save the American Family' White?"

The image of the Reverend White, blurry under a Buzzfeed headline I'd scanned a while ago, popped into my brain. "Oh my God."

"Exactly. God!" Thomas pointed excitedly at the ceiling, "Here!" He pointed at the ground.

I jumped up from my toadstool. "Did you see the crosses this morning?"

"I did," Thomas said. "My grade didn't get hit though."

Thomas peered into his kale chips bag in search of whatever you would expect to find in a kale chip bag. "Wouldn't it be so much nicer if instead of a cross they gave you a present? Like, 'Hey, here's just something for you because I think you're special.' Like a Jesus sweater. I would wear a Jesus sweater, if it was tasteful."

"I'd wear anything that's not 'Your parents are gay, you're going to hell.' That's White's thing, right?" I'd only seen the one article.

"Probably," Thomas said, "after a while most of them blend into one big blob of bigotry, to be honest."

"Until they move to your town." And suddenly I wasn't hungry anymore.

"Right," Thomas said. "So. Anyway, a new local celebrity. More YouTube famous than famous famous, but still. Exciting."

"I guess." My stomach started to twist.

Thomas flipped his phone out of his bag. "We should look up his videos. Could be good Mystery Club material."

"No."

"No?" Thomas tilted his head back into his throne, deep in thought. "You know, I assumed it was this White kid who put the crosses on the lockers, but that seems a little obvious, doesn't it? Do you think it was the allied forces?"

There's a Students' Christian Alliance here, formerly run by Harley Car, actual name. It was currently seeking new leadership because Mr. and Mrs. Car split up and Harley moved to Las Vegas with his mom.

"Maybe," I said.

"Hard to imagine them organizing in advance without new management. Are the crosses still there?"

"I don't know."

"Hey!" Naoki said, marching down the auditorium aisle like a majorette. "Are you eating fries and talking about stuff?" She grinned.

"Some of us are not eating fries," Thomas said, shaking his kale snack.

"Yeah," I sighed.

Naoki jumped up onto the stage and looked at Thomas. "Some of us are a little on edge today," Thomas added.

"Oh," Naoki said quietly. "I see. Ready for bio, Monty?"

I stood up. "Yes. I have to go do something first."

\* \* \*

As I walked down the hall, my heart hammering in my head like a car alarm, I could see the rows of crosses ahead. Still there. *Glad the administration is all over it*, I thought.

Guess it wasn't a huge priority for the staff to remove a *cross*. Because, you know, what's the big deal?

*It's not the end of the world or anything,* a voice in my head fumed. *Right? It's just someone tagging someone's locker with a religious figure? Who doesn't love a Jesus on a cross?*

It took two regular pencils, a mechanical pencil, and a ballpoint pen, but I eventually pried the thing off my locker. The stream of post-lunch kids slowed to a crawl behind me, slowing down the way you do at a car accident. I could hear Naoki in the background talking but not what she was saying.

Then, right before I wrenched it off, I could swear I heard someone chuckling. But I spun around, and it was just Naoki.

"You okay?" she asked.

"Let's just go."

The cross left a huge navy hole in the paint of my locker. It looked like someone had cracked it with a cannonball.

"You want to go home maybe?" Naoki whispered.

"No, I'm fine. It's fine." The tips of my fingers were all raw. I shoved the cross into my bag and stomped to class.

It wasn't hard to spot Kenneth White, son of the Reverend White, in bio. I mean, all I had to do was look for someone I didn't know. I tried not to stare as Naoki and I made our way to our spots, until I was behind him and better able to glare freely.

He was football-tall and stocky, with a big, wide neck. His hair was so blond it was almost see-through. It looked like doll hair. When he turned to look out the window, I could practically see his veins.

"That's Kenneth White?" I whispered.

Naoki nodded. "Yes, it is. He's in my Spanish class as well."

He looked as if someone had chipped him out of marble.

We spent the class drawing cells. Naoki drew hers with the faintest pencil line, thinner than an eyelash.

"Your cells look like ghosts," I whispered, pointing.

Naoki looked down at her sheet of paper. "Do ghosts have cells?"

Something about having Kenneth White in the room made my head hurt. Maybe it was how hard I was staring at the back of his head.

The bell rang and students started jumping out of their seats, slinging bags over shoulders. Shouting across the room. Stuff like, "Wait up, *dick!*"

I felt light-headed and heavy all at the same time.

Kenneth stood, like some sort of Neolithic creature, propping his hands on the desk and shoving his chair back. He must have been over six feet tall. He practically had to unfold himself to get out from under the desk. He was wearing leather boots like the kind construction workers wear, neatly tied up tight. Not like some sort of cool hipster thing. Like someone planning on digging a hole or something.

A hole for sinners.

I didn't want to get out of my chair. I kind of wanted to crawl under my desk.

I mean, seriously, it's one thing to have a school full of idiots to deal with; it's something else entirely to have to sit with someone who you know, for a fact, thinks you're going to hell.

So I just sat for a bit. Feeling like lead and staring at Kenneth's now empty seat.

"Hey," Naoki said, touching my shoulder lightly with her finger. "What are you doing after school?"

I swung my head back in a gesture that might have looked a little psychotic. "Ah. Nothing, I guess."

Slipping her stuff into her bag, Naoki smiled. "Why don't you come over, and we'll watch a documentary? Or just have a snack."

Clearly there is something medicinal for me about the word *snack*.

"Do you have frozen yogurt?" I asked.

"I'll make some," Naoki said, rubbing her hands together. "I can totally do that."

* * *

Naoki's house smells like Japanese food. Maybe that's a little racist to say, because her mother is Japanese Canadian and her dad is Cree. I'm not saying I think all Japanese people have houses that smell like soy sauce. Plus I think it's an amazing smell, and I love that it hits you as soon as you walk in the door. Both her parents travel a lot, so her house is usually empty. Her dad is a famous sculptor, and her mom directs documentaries. Naoki says she likes to be alone so it doesn't really bother her. Which I totally get because sometimes I just want, like, five minutes of uninterrupted me time without a knock on the door asking me how I am and if I want something.

Or, *Have you seen your sister's socks?*

We walked in the door, and she dumped her bag and kicked off her little black ballet flats onto a little kitten-shaped mat.

"Now," she said, grabbing my bag and tossing it in the same pile as hers, "what should we put in our frozen yogurt?"

Coconut. Oreos. Avocado. Greek yogurt. Soy milk. Honey. Ice.

All whipped up into a masterpiece I ate out of a little purple-and-yellow rice bowl with a little pink spoon shaped like a rose petal.

"Where do you get this stuff?" I gasped, turning the spoon over in my hand.

Naoki smiled. "My dad makes most of it. Also, his family does ceramics. So they send us things every year."

We sat in her dad's garden on these two massive beanbag chairs. I lay back and felt the day kind of wipe away with every bite of cold white and green.

"Would you rather see the future clearly or have a perfect memory of the past?" Naoki asked, reaching out to run her finger along the leaf of some crazy alien-looking plant I'd never seen before.

I paused to suck on my petal spoon to think and to savor the joy of homemade frozen yogurt. "See the future. Definitely. Oh yeah, I told you about the Eye of Know, right?"

"You did, just a tiny bit," Naoki said, burrowing deeper into her beanbag chair so it swallowed her up like a cocoon. "It sounds like the name of a book of magic."

We squished our beanbags together, and I tried to find a picture of it on the Internet, but the site wouldn't load on my phone. So I drew the Eye on a page I ripped out of the back of my bio textbook.

"So it's like a mirror," Naoki said, balancing the drawing carefully on the flat of her palm, like it was some sort of ancient artifact.

"No," I said. "I mean, it's for seeing, but I think it's for seeing, like, other things. I mean, I read the description as gaining knowledge into things that people . . . like regular people . . . can't see."

"Which is a lot of things," Naoki said, raising her eyebrows.

The first time we met Naoki, Thomas and I had only been doing the Mystery Club for a year or so. We were sitting in the clubs room, arguing about *Doctor Who*, which Thomas thought was an appropriate subject to discuss in the Mystery Club and I did not.

"I mean the *original Doctor Who*, Montgomery, not any of these new impostors," Thomas charged.

"It doesn't *matter*, Thomas. And it depresses me to think you're drawing a distinction."

"This level of rigidity doesn't suit you, Montgomery."

"It's a *mystery* club, not a crappy TV club, Thomas."

"Take that back right now or I will *wal—*"

And Naoki just knocked on the door. And we both sat up in our chairs, like, "Uh, hello?"

Naoki stepped into the room, like some curious alien descending from its ship onto the crusty desert sand, her body draped in what looked like a silver parachute, her hair, which was black then, tied up in blue ribbons. And I think she said, "Did you say this is a Mystery Club?"

"Yah," I said.

"Good." She walked in and sat down. "I'm here for the mystery."

Like, at no point did Naoki think she was going to see a club that would involve reading whodunits.

It's like she knew she was walking into a different kind of mystery. And that was why she walked in.

Naoki believes that nothing is random. Like, technically there's actually this thing called probability, which is a math thing that tells you what the possibility is of something happening, like rolling a die and getting a two. Naoki's basic theory is, yeah, sure, there's math, but on top of it, there's this un-math. In Naoki's un-math, everything happens not because of math but because of stronger, often inexplicable forces pulling things this way and that.

Which is kind of interesting because Naoki's also really good at math.

It was kind of perfect, I thought, that I would find something like the Eye of Know now, when I knew someone like Naoki. Someone who would actually (a) think that something like the Eye of Know was possible and (b) think it was cool.

After we finished our yogurt, we watched a video about cats that can smell cancer, which is also on my list of mysterious things.

☺ Extra-sensory powers of pets

Around us, crickets chirped. The wind chimes Naoki's dad made out of clay clinked and clanked.

63

There was a rap on the patio door, and Naoki's tiny mother, who I swear is, like, three feet tall and looks a little bit like that fashion designer in that movie from Pixar, tapped her watch. Dinner.

"I better motor," I sighed, rolling out of my bean bag.

"Okay, well." Naoki stood. At her feet was a figure eight drawn out in little stones. Which I hadn't even noticed she was doing. At the door, she smiled a big smile. "Hey. I just want to say, I'm glad you are my friend, Montgomery. I'll see you tomorrow."

I felt my smile pull at my face, which was clearly kind of an unfamiliar shape for my face to make. "Thanks! Me too!"

*How is it Naoki is just so nice?* I wondered. It seemed so easy for her. Even when people treated her like some sort of ditz at school. It was like she just didn't care. Like it wasn't important.

I could have taken the bus home, but it was so nice I decided to walk. It's twenty minutes if I walk fast. Plus I wanted to add some stuff to my app before I forgot, and I can't type and ride the bus, because it makes me nauseous.

☺ Random vs. non-random things or coincidences
☺ The Eye of Know and how it works and whether it lets you see through time

I licked my lips. They still tasted like coconut.

☺ Why homemade fro-yo is better than Yoggy's

I cut through the park and ran up the slide and down the slide and just felt kind of amazing. Which was amazing considering what a crap day it was. Which I tried not to think about.

By the time I got back, the house was totally quiet. Like, still.

*Soccer practice*, I thought.

The only light on in the whole house was the one over the dining room table. It glowed like a beacon.

I turned the corner.

The box, placed in the center of the table, was brown and scuffed, like some kind of ancient package rescued from a war effort, scratched and torn at the edges. It was about as big as a shoe box cut in half. Perfectly square.

I spun it around. Taped to the outside was an envelope, with a printed card that read:

---

TO: Montgomery Sole
FROM: **Manchester Technology**
*Please enjoy the enclosed EYE OF KNOW!*
*Every great adventure begins with a new discovery.*
*Please read your EYE OF KNOW instructions carefully.*
*Thank you for shopping with Manchester. We hope you'll visit our site again soon!*

---

"Oh my gosh!" I grabbed the box and rocketed up the stairs, stumbling through the darkness, slamming on light switches. I burst into my room and closed the door, even though no one was home.

Sitting on my bed, I tore it open.

There, nested in a handful of crinkly brown paper stuffing, was . . . the Eye of Know?

It . . . wasn't white. But black. Solid. Black.

"What the eff?"

Was this going to be more or less disappointing than the book of spells I'd ordered for $10.99 that had ended up being a blank book *for writing spells in*, instead of a book of actual magical spells?

*Hard to say*, I thought, foraging through the rest of the packaging.

The only other thing in the box was a little white pamphlet of instructions, which was really more of a folded card, like a greeting card. On the cover, it read:

In sight
not see

On the inside, the left side had a drawing of an eyeball, with the eye open. And a picture of a black rectangle.

On the right side was a picture of an eye colored black, and a white rectangle.

On the back, in writing that was kind of fuzzy, was this:

*black light*
*not be*

I flipped the card over and back.

*In sight*
*not see*
*black light*
*not be*

Tossing the card, I picked up the stone and held it to the light. It was the shape of a domino but without the little dots on it.

The cord was just a piece of white string.

"Wow," I said to my empty room, the den of disappointment. "Not even an adjustable leather strap!"

I flipped the rock over in my palm. It was perfectly black. No cracks or little white flecks. Nothing. Against my skin, it looked like this perfect black hole. Like there was an actual rectangular hole in my hand. A doorway to some sort of endless darkness.

"Okay, so," I said, this time to the stone, possibly. "Time for great insight."

I closed my fingers around the stone and squeezed it a little.

Thinking back to my extensive research, I closed my eyes and tried to arrange my thoughts like I was setting a table.

Clear away everything else. Away, math. Away, TV. Away, thoughts about food.

What did I want to know?

"Kenneth White," I whispered.

*Come on, Eye. Kenneth White—what is he up to? What horrors will he bring to Jefferson High?*

*Trouble?*

*Yes or no?*

The stone sat silent in my hand.

I heard, felt nothing.

*Okay,* I thought. *This time I'll just clear my mind. See what shows up.*

I sat up on my bed. Crossed my legs. Cleared my mind. *Now.*

. . .

Nothing.

My first absolute blank mind in forever. Quiet as a pillow.

And nothing.

I opened my eyes and the Eye of Know stared blankly at me.

Suddenly there was the distinct racket of two soccer moms and a soccer kid piling into the front door.

*"Mon-ty!* Is this your mess?"

"Mamaaaaaa! Monty ate my fro-yo!"

"There's another one in the freezer!" I screamed.

"There's only banana!" Tesla howled.

"Monty, come here and clean up these dishes!"

*"Geez!"* I yelled, carefully placing the Eye in my bag. "Coming!"

*Ping!*

On the computer there were two messages from Thomas.

Thomas: Are you there?

Thomas: I'm watching Back to the Future on Netflix. Golden oldies! You'd hate it. It's not witchy at all. But this guy, whoever he is, is CUTE cute cute.

# 5

☺ Messages you find—in food or possibly in other
  inanimate objects
☺ People who can talk to objects and hear their his-
  tories (only a TV thing?)
☺ Mind control

I'M OFF AND ON ABOUT THE WHOLE MYSTERIOUS–
messages-from-the-beyond thing, maybe because all the websites on the subject are kind of tired. A lot of what I've found
on the web is about people who see divine images in the things
they eat. Especially toast. Toast is a big medium for spiritual
symbols and portraits, most specifically of the kind relating
to Jesus Christ. I'm not sure why this is. It seems like such a
weird way for a deity to communicate something really important, like a Second Coming. I mean, isn't toast something

you eat in the morning when you're sleepy and not really pay-
ing attention? Wouldn't it be better to put a holy message in
something like a rock? Something that's going to stick around
if you don't notice it the first time? Something that's not going
to go bad if you need to hold on to it for a while?

I found this blog once about how corporations are putting
images into foods as a kind of subliminal messaging system.
It also has instructions on how to home compost, but mostly
it's all these pictures people have taken of food with "dis-
tinctly political" messages in it. There's a picture in there of
a soup stain on this guy's tablecloth that does actually look
like an elephant eating a donkey.

This guy also said government cheese is all implanted with
a chemical that makes people vote Republican.

I told Tiffany about this once, you know, thinking she'd be
concerned as a person working in the food service industry,
and she was basically like, "Yeah, tell me something I don't
know."

Tiffany's theory is that we, that is, us members of Western
society, are constantly having symbolism, in her words,
"crammed down our throats."

"It's everywhere. Messages on what to eat, who to love, what
to buy—all that is pretty much already set in our corporate system and disseminated through everything from television to
pizza," she noted as she grabbed a blueberry from the toppings
bar and sucked it from her fingers to her mouth. "You know
I wrote my thesis on beauty pageants and their connection
to the fast-food industry, right? I told you that, right?"

"Uh," I stammered, staring intently at Tiffany's fingers, which, I had just noticed, did not look like the cleanest in the world. "Do you always eat that stuff with your bare hands?"

"Oh"—Tiffany pressed her hands against her chest—"pardon *me*, Miss Manners. Do you want your free toppings or what?"

There was a moment of silence while Tiffany bored holes into me with her purple-black eyes, and I tried to do as quick an analysis of Tiffany's fingers as possible. *Are they more or less gross than Tesla's hands?* I asked myself, because I eat what Tesla has her fingers all over all the time.

*Less.*

"Free toppings, please," I concluded.

"I thought so."

All this has led me to wonder if maybe there was some connection between bread and Christianity that merited further investigation. Like, was there some commercial thing behind Christians' obsession with bread? Or maybe it was chemical?

☺ Subliminal messages
☺ Hallucinogens

* * *

The next morning, I was swimming in crosses. Everything looked like a cross to me: telephone poles, the plus signs on the blackboard, roads intersecting on my drive to school.

Kenneth White, meanwhile, spent the day vying for the title of Quietest Person in Aunty. Math, silent. Bio, quieter than cement. I can only imagine he ate his lunch in silence, too. Every class, he just sat, slumped, in his seat, his arms folded over his chest. Like he was posing for a painting or something. He never looked around. Never talked to anyone. Just sat there with his book open and his pencil on his notebook.

Staring.

At.

Nothing.

Maybe he was confused because all he did at home was Bible studies. Maybe he was snickering in biology because we were looking at what Mr. Jenner called the building blocks of life, and Christians think the building blocks of life are . . . I'm not sure, actually. Probably not gooey cells, though. Sometimes, I'd sneak a look and he'd be squinting ahead or looking out the window. His face as still as glass.

The only audio evidence of his existence in Aunty was the heavy, rubbery sound of his big boots clomping down the hallway from class to class.

At the Mystery Club meeting after school, Thomas shook up his healthy snack-in-a-bottle (which looked like kale and smelled like garbage). "Those boots are killing me," he moaned. "I mean, he's not a terrible-looking guy. But those *boots*! Puhlease! Those boots are o-ver."

"Yeah, and his dad thinks we're all going to hell," I said, licking the remnants of my snacks of cheesy twists off my fingers.

Thomas paused midshake. "That does not change the fact that his boots are ugly, Montgomery, but thanks for bringing that up, *again*."

It was Thomas's turn to pick a topic for Mystery Club, and so we talked about superpowers and what superpowers Thomas thinks are over- and underrated. Thomas's list of overrated superpowers is very long. Basically anything you've seen any man do in a comic book, he's over it.

"I think we've all had enough of flying, yes?" he said, grabbing a piece of chalk and starting a superhero cartoon sketch on the board. "And lasers."

"I always thought the laser thing was kind of confusing," I added from my semi-prone position on the floor, "because technically a laser should just shoot through a person, but it never does. It just, you know, *zaps*. And pings off things."

"I think it's time we refocused on people who can melt and reform into different objects and creatures," Thomas concluded, stepping back from his drawing. It was a very bumpy superhero.

"Like Jell-O?" Naoki asked, holding her hands out like she was holding a big clump of Jell-O.

"More like lava," Thomas said.

"Doesn't feel very super," I said. "What's so great about dissolving?"

"Did you see *Terminator 2*?" Thomas asked.

Naoki shook her head. "Who's in that?"

"Not all of us are into old-timey movies, Thomas," I groaned.

"The former governor of our great state," Thomas noted, drawing a loose caricature on the board with a single stroke. "Mr. Schwarzenegger."

Naoki shrugged. "He's an actor?"

"Someday," Thomas said, dropping the chalk and dusting off his hands, "I will take you on the Netflix retro tour."

"I'm sure it will be very enlightening," Naoki said, stepping forward to take a closer look at Thomas's sketches. "You're a good drawer."

"Thank you," Thomas cooed, taking up his chalk to write out his keywords on the board. "And so, in conclusion to my conclusion, *survival* and *adaptation*, yes, is as super as it gets, darling. Let's have more melting heroes. It's time. Plus if you can reform into a nice-looking guy in a decent suit . . . *well* then, that's a whole new ballgame, yes?"

"If I had a superpower," Naoki added, walking over to where I was lying on the floor and dropping down into a graceful kneel, "I'd have superhealing."

"What do you want, Monty?" Thomas asked, swinging around to point at me.

I tried to picture myself, landing on a battlefield with a team of superheroes, watching them all pull out their weapons. Ready for the enemy. But still, I thought, you'd never know what was coming at you. It's like rock-paper-scissors. You pull out a rock, someone has paper, you're doomed. "Omnipotence," I said, finally.

"You want to be all-powerful," Thomas asked with a raised eyebrow.

"Oh," I said. "No. What's it called? To know everything."

"Omniscience." Naoki said, tilting her head. "I think that would be tiring. I mean, *everything*. And *knowing* it. You could never go see a movie again."

"No thanks," Thomas said.

"Okay, maybe not everything," I conceded. "Just . . . what's coming at me."

Thomas stood and picked up his bag, which that day was this kind of weird-looking basket like you would expect Mary Poppins to use or something. "So concludes the meeting of the fabulous Mystery Club. And now," he finished, bowing deeply, "I'm off to continue my valiant effort to bring some modicum of culture to Jefferson High."

"Draaaamedy," I droned.

"Dramedy," Naoki repeated, watching Thomas slip out the door. "It's such a funny name. It doesn't feel like a word."

"It's not. *Oh hey!*" I said, reaching into my bag and pulling out the Eye. "Look! It arrived!"

"Oh!" Naoki leaned over and put her face close to the dangling stone. "It's like a mirror, it's so black!"

I sat up and lay the stone flat on my hand. "Yeah," I said. "I guess."

Naoki moved so she was squished right next to me, seeing it from my angle, presumably. "Does it work?"

"Um, I don't know. I haven't really done anything with it yet. I mean, yesterday I tried to see if any of, you know, the typical ESP things would work with it. But nothing really happened."

"Well," Naoki said as she stood and slung her bag over her shoulder, "you're supersmart. You'll figure it out."

"Sure," I said, trying to sound convinced and not just

disappointed. I slipped the stone back into my bag and scrambled to my feet.

In the hallway, Naoki stopped and put her finger on my chest. "You just have to figure out what you need to know," she said. "I bet that's it."

"Could be," I said.

Naoki headed off to her locker, and I turned to head home. *What do I need to know?*

*I mean, maybe it's not about a person*, I thought. *Maybe it's something bigger. Don't I have a whole list of stuff I wanted to know?* I mused, grabbing my phone out of my pocket and scanning through it . . . until I nearly slammed into a wall, much to the amusement of what looked like the football team, and Matt Truit.

*"Nice going!"* some guy in a baseball hat yodeled.

*"Watch your face, Sole!"* Matt hollered. *"Bus-ted!"*

Clearly, knowing the basic layout of the school would be a start.

* * *

I spotted the posters on my way home from school.

## THE REVEREND WHITE WILL SAVE YOU

They were everywhere, on telephone poles and mailboxes all over, colorful, glossy photos of the Reverend White in various poses. The Reverend White had white hair and wore white suits. In the pictures, he had his arms around men and women, presumably couples, some of them with babies.

# WE WILL SAVE
# THE AMERICAN FAMILY,
# TOGETHER.

The Reverend White looked down at me from every corner.

"We will save you," he said. He sounded so confident in my head.

I stood on the street corner, California breeze brushing past me as I looked up at him.

*Save me or save this town from people like me?* I thought. *Save me or destroy me?*

*Destroy you.*

*Oh yeah?*

I spent the next two hours running from telephone pole to telephone pole, ripping down every poster I could find. He was everywhere, staring at me as I reached up and tore him in half. I needed the superpower of a million Reverend White poster-seeking hands. Until then, one at a time.

# THE REVEREND WHITE IS HERE TO SAVE YOU!

*Riiiiiiip!*

When I got home, I still had two of the posters balled up in my pocket. The house was humming. As soon as I opened the door, I was flooded by the smell of fatty saltiness, chicken and potatoes. I could hear Momma Jo throwing around pots and pans. I tried to let the door click closed as quietly as possible.

"Set the table, whoever that is!" Momma Jo yelled over the rattle of chopping.

"Special dinner night," Tesla added, her voice bouncing. She was doing jumping jacks in front of the TV in the living room.

"Why don't you set the table?" I asked, kicking off my boots into the chaotic pile of shoes that is our doorway.

"She asked *you*," Tesla snapped as she switched to a kind of high-knee running on the spot. She had a little warm-up outfit on. Pink and green stripes. Like a Christmas elf.

Sometimes it's hard to believe that Tesla and I have the same mom egg and uterus and the same sperm donor. Tesla looks like the angel to my devil. I've got straight black-brown hair that hangs long and wouldn't keep a curl if I glued one in there. Tesla's got this crazy almost-red curly hair that she's always fighting to keep in a ponytail, with, like, a million plastic bands and barrettes. Tesla's a ball of energy. Everything she does has bounce. I don't think it's even possible for her to tiptoe. Like, even if she wanted to.

Last year we got our pictures taken for Mama Kate's birthday, and the photographer spent, like, an hour telling Tesla how much she looked like all these different movie stars.

"What are you? You're like a young Susan Sarandon. You know who that is? Smile for the camera there, Susan!"

Tesla had smiled and carefully adjusted the sleeves of her flowery dress. Her favorite.

I think I had on a polyester dress I'd found at a yard sale, and I was wearing it because it didn't have a rip. And I'd been specifically told I could not wear anything with a rip for this timeless memento, which was one of the few things I could do for Mama Kate, who did so much for me. According to Momma Jo.

"I'm not saying you have to wear a doily, Monty," Momma Jo had grumbled, picking through my stack of clothes. "I'm just saying . . . *hey*, is this my sweater? What are you doing with all my stuff?"

At the photographer's studio, as I leaned on a giant prop foam heart, the photographer had smiled. "Oh," he had added, gesturing toward me, just as he was about to snap the last picture, "and you, big sister, you look . . . very grown up."

"Just take the picture," I'd grimaced, pulling at the tight sleeves on my dress.

Of course, I have no interest in looking like a celebrity. I think celebrity culture is basically a waste of time.

That, and my aversion to buying any clothes new from a retail chain has led most people at my school to think I'm either a Goth or a hippie. Which is hilarious to me. Because if any of them would actually do any research on either of those two things, they would see I'm not either.

I'm not buying into a look. I'm refusing to conform to most people's obsession with looks.

"I'm nothing," I told Thomas once.

"You're just you in your momma's clothes," he retorted. "You're a teenager dressed as a lesbian in her forties. Bravo."

Back at the house, which smelled more and more fried by the second, Tesla dropped to the floor and started crunches.

"First of all," I countered, moving from the doorway of

shoes to the carpet so I could stand over her, "she didn't ask me. She said 'whoever.'"

"She said 'whoever,' but that *means* you," Tesla huffed, crunching. "I can't set the table. I'm training."

"For the Olympics? A noble quest?"

"It's Tesla's big game tomorrow!" Mama Kate said as she jogged down the stairs. "Semi-regional girls' junior soccer championship game tomorrow."

*Right.*

I think it always kind of, sort of bummed my moms out that I'm not, in any way, shape, or form, into any kind of sports.

Not even archery. Not even bowling. Not even *darts*.

My moms are sporty people. They hike, they bike, they ski, they rock climb, they play lesbian baseball every first Thursday of the month. Momma Jo was a professional field hockey player when she was younger, field hockey being this weird sport where people play hockey on grass instead of ice.

My moms met at an international lesbian intramural sports tournament. When Mama Kate sprained her ankle in a soccer game, Momma Jo drove her to the hospital. Just because. And that was it. Mama Kate even left her college so they could go to the same school in Canada.

Then they moved back here when Momma Jo's company opened an office in California.

I asked Momma Jo once if there was some category for that on the sperm donor form. Like, if there was a box you could check for *sporty* or *athletic*. Momma Jo said the only boxes they cared about were *human* and *male*.

"It's not sperm that makes you sporty," she added. "Trust me, I know."

The best evidence for this would be Tesla, who is made from the exact same genetic stuff as me and is *super*sporty. Every month, it seems, it's a different sport and a different team and a different animal. In the fall, during soccer season, it was all about the Namaste Yoga Studio Cubs, because that's who sponsors soccer teams in California, yoga studios. Sorbetties.

*"Dinner!"* Momma Jo howled, banging on a pot with her big wooden spoon.

Tesla hopped up and bounded into the dining room. I strolled. Because it's not a race and I, unlike Tesla, do not feel the need to be exercising every minute of the day.

I love our dining room. One year for Christmas my moms decided we should repaint it so it was more festive. So the walls are red stripes (Momma), lavender (Mama), pink (Tesla), and black and blue stars (me). Plus all our plates are from garage sales and antique places, Mama Kate's obsession, so they're all different. I always make sure I get the red bowl with the bull's-eye in the middle. Mama Kate found it on my birthday last year.

So anyway, there we were, eating Tesla's favorite night-before-the-big-game meal, deep-fried chicken burgers, sweet potato fries, potato salad, and beans, like a regular lesbian family.

"So what's the name of the other team?" I asked.

"The Canyon Tires Elementary Crows."

"Tough team?"

"Uh, *yes*." Tesla pushed her plate back. "So I think we should pray. To win."

"What?" I coughed.

Momma Jo, who has a big laugh, dropped her chicken burger and laughed big. "You think that's the tiebreaker?"

Tesla frowned. I laughed. Mama frowned. Mama Kate is super into the idea that you shouldn't laugh at kids unless they're telling you a joke.

Momma Jo dropped her fork and put her hands in the air. "Okay, okay! Look. It's not a bad idea, Tesla. I just, I think what I'm saying is . . . What? I'm saying praying doesn't win games. Praying is something people do as part of something much bigger, like a religion."

Mama Kate put her hand on Tesla's hand. "What we're trying to say is, sweetie, praying is not something you do *just* so you can win a game."

"No kidding," I murmured, two fries in my mouth.

"Other people are praying," Tesla protested, folding her arms over her chest, pushing her lips into an angry knot.

"Tesla," Mama Kate sighed.

Tesla banged her fist on the table. "Abigail's parents are praying. Caitlin's parents are praying. Sarah's parents are praying. Pearl's parents are praying. If they all pray and I don't pray, we could *lose*."

"Well," Momma Jo said, "they're probably praying because their parents pray as part of their religious practice."

"Why don't *we* have a religious practice?" Tesla cried.

"We don't need one," I snapped.

"Maybe we *do* need one," Tesla snapped back.

"I'm going to get dessert," Mama Kate said, and she picked up her plate and pushed out her chair.

"I don't want any." Tesla pouted.

I watched Mama Kate disappear into the kitchen, kind of bent over a bit like she was searching the floor for a lost quarter.

"Why don't you just chill out?" I hissed.

"Why don't you just mind your own business?" Tesla hissed back.

Momma Jo looked at my black and blue stars. "Montgomery. Enough. Tesla. There are lots of things that different families do differently. This is one of them. Some people eat certain dishes, some people wear different clothes, some people go to church, some people have two dads . . ."

"Who has two dads?" Tesla huffed.

"Elton John's kids," I piped in, my mouth still partly full of fries.

"Shut up, Monty," Tesla barked.

"Ricky Martin's kids," I added, pointing another fry at Tesla.

"*Mon-teeee!*" Tesla jumped out of her chair and pointed an angry finger at me across the table. "*Shut up!*"

"Montgomery," Momma Jo said, her voice like a hammer. A slightly tired hammer.

In the kitchen, pots and pans rattled. I could just see Mama Kate, leaning on the counter.

"Excuse me," I said, slamming my knife down on the table, which was louder than I wanted it to be. "First of all, how come she gets to tell me to shut up? Second, how come Tesla gets to act like a little brat just because she's not allowed to *pray*? Maybe there are bigger things than *soccer games*, Tesla. And just because everyone in this stupid town thinks you should pray, *Tesla*, doesn't mean you have to do it. Grow up!"

"*Shut up, Monty!*"

"*You shut up!*"

"*Enough!*" Momma Jo banged the table with her palm.

There was a crashing sound in the kitchen, plates fighting in the sink.

"I'm outta here." And, of course, by "outta here" I meant, "I'm going to my room."

Because, at sixteen, I can't just charge off into the sunset. Just to my room. A place to contemplate why it is I shouldn't yell at my sister. Even though she is being an idiot.

Tesla is the only person I currently know who's been a kid with two moms her whole life, too.

And most of the time she's the dumbest person I've ever met.

Like, why does she want to *pray* now?

I tried to imagine Tesla standing in whatever it is they call that space by the soccer field where the teams sit, with all her friends. And her friends being like, "We should all pray." Maybe there was even some kid who told the other players that our moms don't pray because they're lesbians.

How stupid is it to have to explain why it's so much more complicated than that?

I lay down on my bed and looked at the ceiling.

Mama Kate's parents are really religious. Evangelicals.

Believers in the Second Coming. When we were little, they would give Tesla and me religious-type stuff all the time. Like, for our birthdays they would send us books like *Good Christian Girls* tucked into the covers of regular books. They slipped little gold crosses into birthday cards signed, *Jesus loves you.* Once they sent us cards of Jesus where you could shift the card and he would look up at the sky, the thorns on his head twinkling.

Tesla was so little when most of this was happening. She'd just fold them up into her dollhouses or cut them into snowflakes. She called them "man cards."

When I was little, I thought Jesus was, like, this person my grandparents knew. Like a great-uncle. Great-Uncle Jesus from Kansas.

Typically, as soon as they were unwrapped, Mama Kate would swoop in, take the presents away. Promise to take us to the store and get us something else. Then she'd go into the kitchen, sit at the table, call her parents.

"Yes, but I'm *asking* you to stop, Mom. Yes. I know. Okay, well, we don't do that in our family. *Yes,* I do have a family, Mom. Dad, I'm not talking about it. *No.* Yes, I do, Dad. Mom. I'm going to hang up now. I do love you. Goodbye."

While Mama Kate talked, I would sit outside the kitchen door, my fingers tucked under the metal threshold that separated the carpet from the tile, and wait for her to hang up the phone. Then I would go in and make sure she was okay.

The room was always so quiet and still after those phone calls. I could feel the fridge and the lights vibrating under my feet. "Mama?"

Sometimes she'd wipe her eyes with the corner of the table-cloth or her sleeve.

Sometimes she'd look at the ceiling. Sometimes there would be tears when she looked at me. "Hey, sweetie. Do you want a snack?"

Why is it so earth-shatteringly scary to see your parent cry? It's like the worst weapon in the world. Like the worst kind of kryptonite. "Is everything okay, Mama?"

"Oh. Sure, sweetie," she'd say, her voice all wobbly. "I'm just sad. Not too sad. But sad."

Once when I was six, after a really bad phone call, Mama Kate went to bed and didn't come out for dinner. So I made her a heart of Rice Krispies treats, which I stuck to her door, piece by piece. Because you can do that with Rice Krispies treats. Kids at school did it all the time.

Of course, most kids at school weren't dealing with a particularly nasty infestation of ants. Who apparently love Rice Krispies treats.

"Don't worry about it," Momma Jo said, even though ants are one of her least-favorite things. "You tried to do a nice thing, so it's okay. Weird but okay."

That whole week it was Momma Jo, not Mama Kate, who came and picked me up from school. Because Mama Kate was feeling bad, she said.

It was the first and only time I ever dreaded seeing Momma Jo. Because it meant something was wrong.

It wasn't always that bad. Mostly, Mama Kate would just get a little sad and then we'd have frozen yogurt together.

Sometimes we would just get a spoon of frozen yogurt and share it. Mama Kate said ice cream was the best treat when you were feeling bad because you could just feel everything melting away.

"I am going to stop them from calling," I told her once, not sure how I would do that. "I'm going to take all our phones."

"You don't have to worry about that," Mama Kate said. "Just eat your fro-yo. See how it's sweet on your tongue? Then gone? It's like magic."

*  *  *

There was a knock on the door. Momma Jo's knock. Two hard raps.

"Monty?"

"Yeah?"

She opened the door a crack. "All right. So. No one should tell you to shut up. Yes? But we're a family. We need to support each other. Tesla's your little sister and sometimes she needs the big-sister kind of support."

"Okay," I said, not moving from my prone position on the bed. I'd wedged myself between many rejected sofa pillows, removed from the living room over the years, to form my bedroom nest.

Momma Jo leaned on the door. "Tesla's game is at four thirty. I want you to be there. Montgomery? Are you listening to me?"

"Yeah, okay, I'll go." Still not moving. Still like a log. In the wrong, yes, a little, but still offended. So. Not moving.

"Okay," Momma Jo said, slowing closing the door, possibly waiting for some movement. "Good night."

Sometimes when Tesla and I are fighting really bad, Momma Jo will tell me the story of how Tesla and I used to hug all the time. Like, I used to hug and carry her around the house, her feet dragging on the carpet. I don't know when we stopped.

I kicked some cushions off the bed and rolled onto my back. The house was quiet. Just a little bit of a murmur from the TV downstairs. I grabbed the stone from my bag and the card from my desk.

*In sight*
*not see*

[flip]

*black light*
*not be*

*Not be?*
*Not be* what?
Not be dealing with all this crap anymore, maybe.
Dangling the Eye in front of me, I could see my face in the stone.
*Eye know*, I said to my dangling reflection.
And then I just felt ridiculously dorky, so I put it around my neck and tried to pretend I hadn't just been sitting in my bed talking to a rock I ordered on the Internet.

# 6

BREAKFAST WAS POWER PANCAKES WITH THIS WEIRD
nutty wheat thing that actually makes my stomach a little rest-
less, so I only had three.

That morning I'd IM-ed with Naoki about the Eye of Know
and about healing crystals, which was something Naoki's mom
was super into, and Naoki was going to do a whole thing on it
at our next Mystery Club.

Naoki: Was talking to my mom. Is your Eye thing made of
onyx?
Me: Don't think so. Don't know what it is.
Naoki: If you bring it again, I'll bring my necklace my dad
gave me. It's onyx and obsidian.
Me: Cool!

☺ Healing crystals!

While Tesla was screaming about her socks, I took the Eye off my neck and let it dangle in the sunlight. A black hole.

It wasn't a bad-looking stone. Maybe it would end up being just a nice piece of jewelry or something. Maybe it was onyx. That would be nice.

*"Mama!"*

*"Tesla, you are responsible for your own two feet!"*

I slipped the Eye of Know into my bag and bolted down the stairs.

\* \* \*

It was "Support Your Clubs and Teams Day" at school, so the front steps were flooded with club and sports reps, rallying support. Cheerleaders were handing out flyers for upcoming club frivolities. A girl from the Dramedy Club dressed in a fifties skirt was trying to get more kids to sign up for auditions.

"There's a make-out scene," she called coyly to a group of boys at the bottom of the steps, twirling her skirt for extra make-out-possibility emphasis.

I wondered what Thomas, Mr. Patron of the Arts, would think of that.

First period, Kenneth White clomped in after the bell rang and sat in the front row, right corner.

"Mr. White?" Mr. Deever, sweating in a cable-knit sweater,

wandered over to the chalkboard and tapped it with his ruler.

"Yes, sir?" Kenneth said, barely moving a muscle beyond the ones in his lips.

Deever tapped the board. "Care to answer one of these for us? Help us out?"

Kenneth uncurled himself from his seat. It looked as if it took effort. Guy was frickin' tall. "Yes, sir."

*Clomp, clomp, clomp.*

Surprisingly, Kenneth White's handwriting was tiny. Like typewriter tiny. It was like watching a computer solve for "x" on the chalkboard.

Then he handed the chalk back to Mr. Deever and *clomp-clomp*ed back to his seat.

Stone-faced.

Deever surveyed and whistled. "Well done, Kenneth," he marveled. "You have impeccable penmanship. The students of Jefferson could learn a thing or two from you, I think."

Kenneth's face was still as ice. "Thank you, sir."

Then he folded his arms across his chest and, presumably, stopped breathing.

*It's like watching a robot,* I thought, singing myself a little song in my head. *Kid robot! Kid Christian Robot! Fighting sin and doing math! KID ROBOT!*

"Miss Sole!" Mr. Deever barked, banging his stick on the chalkboard. "Care to join us?"

☺ Handwriting and personality—art of reading a
   signature

In English, I overheard Madison Marlow saying the Reverend White was setting up a new church in California, and he
was scouting out locations. Someone else said they heard him
on the radio.

"I thought he got sued," Miffy said. "Right, Madison?"

"That's right. My mom says he's fighting it because it's his
freedom of speech," Madison said, tapping her nails on the
desk. "It's not right the way people on the so-called right have
made freedom a crime in this country."

"You don't say," I whispered.

Apparently, the Reverend White was spreading the word
about the "plague."

"My mom said, if there's a plague, it's probably in California," Madison continued. "My mom says it's nice to have a little
spirit back in the state."

Also, Madison thought Kenneth was an albino.

"Totally." Miffy nodded. "He has that albino look, you
know?"

*Wow*, I thought, *so much insight in English class today*. It was a
little hard to take in all at once.

Still. I made a mental note of two new possible topics.

☺ Albinos: characteristics or special powers?
☺ Head shape and personality

"Can I help you, Montgomery?" Madison snapped, narrowing her gaze, making me wonder if her mascara-gooped eyelashes would connect and fuse her eyes shut.

"You could cut someone with that gaze," I wanted to tell her.

"Oh I'm just sitting here," I said instead, randomly flipping through the pages of my book. "You know, looking up stuff about *darkness*, in my cool rock T-shirt."

I did get a look at Kenneth on my way to chemistry. I couldn't tell from the back if he was an albino or just really blond. It was hard to get a close look at him generally because he was usually up and out of class before I even got a chance to look at his face.

At lunch, we laid Naoki's onyx necklace and my mystery stone out on the lawn.

"It doesn't look like the onyx," Naoki said. "It's weird, because they're both black, but the Eye looks darker."

"I know," I breathed.

Thomas leaned over and peered at the two necklaces. "Naoki's will go better with a blazer," he said finally, "mostly because it doesn't have a *string* for a strap."

"Yeah, it said it would have an adjustable strap," I said. "I think it said it would be leather."

Thomas sniffed. "I'm all for mystery but I have to say, that's what you get for buying something from one of your weird sites. Next thing you know it will be tinfoil hats."

"Hey, if you're in for the mystery, you're open to any and all possibilities," I countered.

Honestly, for someone obsessed with superheroes and astrology, Thomas could be such a cynic sometimes. "I'm just offering my aesthetic opinion," Thomas said, pressing his fingers into his chest in a very *moi?* pose. "I leave the science of this to you two."

"It's a cool name," Naoki added. "The Eye of Know."

"Well," I said, sinking just a tiny bit, "it's not really letting me know anything yet."

Naoki picked up her necklace and strung it back around her neck. "Well, even if it isn't onyx, and even if nothing has happened *yet*, you should wear it," she said. "See what you can see."

Then she popped up off the blanket and raced to fit in flute practice before class.

"Did you even know she played the flute?" Thomas marveled, watching Naoki as she skipped back to school.

"She's a mystery," I said, folding what was left of my French fry lunch into my mouth.

"Oh." Thomas turned and pressed his hand onto mine. "Speaking of which, I don't think I can come to your soccer game adventure. I've got a date."

I raised an eyebrow. "With The Butcher?"

"With The Soprano," Thomas said, straightening his shirtsleeves, which I noticed were looking especially ruffled today.

"Mob?" I asked.

"Puh-lease," Thomas scoffed, lying back with a dramatic harrumph. "As if we date *mobsters*."

"We?"

"He's an opera singer," Thomas said, rolling onto his side

and patting the grass next to him. "Now, let's enjoy some sun before we go back into your version of the lion's den."

"Okay."

We lay back on the grass and discussed how the date might go depending on how good-looking and old the guy turned out to be. The sky was that pulsing electric blue that it is here. It's this unforgettable, I'm-so-blue-it-hurts blue that I've always found kind of ridiculous. It's blue like nail polish for club kids. Anyway, today I wasn't really minding it.

You could hear kids blasting music from their rides in the parking lot.

*Bump, bump, waaaaahhhhh.*

"*Hey!*" a voice called.

I tipped my head up. Somewhere in the glare of the sun stood Matt, twirling a football on one finger. "Nice pants, Thomasssss."

"Thanks." Thomas kept his head tilted back into the sun. We could hear the crunch of many feet on the crispy grass. It was Matt plus posse. I sat up.

Matt tossed a football backward over his shoulder, and some kid dove to catch it. "Where did you get them? Oh my gosh. Was it H&M?" Matt pressed the tips of his fingers to his shoulder. In this sort of girlie pose, I guess. The boys behind him snickered.

"Why do you ask?" Thomas sat up and popped his sunglasses up on top of his head.

"Oh," Matt lisped, "I'm just soooo curioussss. The fabric is fabulous. Ssssso luxurious . . ."

Thomas's face was like a mannequin's. He has this expression he can hold—it's like a supermodel's face when they walk down the runway. Like an *I'm fabulous, what are you?* face.

Matt's lips were twitching with glee.

"You know . . . I think my *sister* has the *same pair*," he said, the words sliding thick off his tongue. "What a *stunning* coincidence."

One of the boys behind Matt slapped his knee and jogged in a little circle, like it was so funny he needed to run it out. Thomas shrugged.

"I see," he said. "Well, your sister has great taste, then."

I looked up at Matt, just standing there. Smiling. He winked at Thomas, turned on his heel. Started walking away.

Matt. Somehow the Matt Truits are not the people we're being saved from, but the people we're supposed to, like, aspire to be. Maybe only because it means you won't have to get crapped on.

"Your sister's fat ass would never fit into these pants," I said.

"I heard that, Sole," Matt shouted over his shoulder.

Thomas turned and raised an eyebrow. "Does he have a sister?"

"I don't know."

"Oh," Thomas said, "I thought . . ."

"I only hung out with him for, like, a week, Thomas."

Thomas gave me a conciliatory pat on the back. "That's what happens when your best friends get strep throat, huh?"

"Sucked all around. Make sure it doesn't happen again."

He stood and brushed the grass off his actually-really-nice velvet pants.

"That guy is such a prick," I said, grabbing a handful of grass and throwing it in Matt's direction. "I hate him."

"Doesn't mean you should say crap about his potentially fictional sister."

"Whatever." I grabbed another handful and tossed it softly at Thomas.

"Okay, well, I love you, babe," he smooched into my ear, and trotted off to class.

I picked up the Eye of Know and put it around my neck. It slid down my chest with what felt like a little pulse.

*See what I see*, I thought. I scooped up my bio notes and tromped off to class.

* * *

By 4:15 p.m., the parking lot and bleachers at Honora Park Soccer Field were packed. The stands were a sea of soccer moms, with their matching coolers of snacks and their yelling faces. They sported fleece vests and hiking shoes, California outdoor gear for all seasons, especially when paired with lightweight baseball caps and sunglasses.

My moms always wear matching vests and shoes to games: red for Momma, lavender for Mama. It's kind of embarrassing, but I kind of like it, too.

The players sprinted up and down the field. Little girls in soccer jerseys—orange for the Cubs, baby blue for the Crows— all pinging around like icons on those old video games people used to play before they had Xbox. Like the *Space Invaders* game I saw this one time at a truck shop that Momma Jo beat me at (four games to one).

The Crows looked mean and determined. And huge.

Tesla sat on the bench, perched next to Mama Kate. At some point she stood up and waved to me in the bleachers. I realized it had been a while since I'd been to one of these things. Hating sports makes supporting your family's obsession a little awkward at times. Or, you know, that's what I've told myself.

As the opening whistle blew, the woman on my left, in Cub orange, pulled out her knitting and thermos, clearly in it for the long haul.

Somewhere downwind, though, another woman was already on her feet, yelling obscenities at the ref. Like, these women called the ref things like the C word. Stuff like that. Bizarre.

You gotta love a yoga-loving hippie mom who lets loose and carnivores out when she hits the soccer field.

I didn't really notice the rest of the people sitting on the other side of me until five minutes into the game, when someone kicked my boots squeezing past. It was a girl in a blue jacket carrying a blue pom-pom.

"Uh, 'scuse me." A girl with her hair in a high top bun gave me a quick up-and-down glance as she stepped over my boots.

There is a way to say "excuse me" that makes it very clear you assume it's the other person's job to move. It was invented by teenagers who hang out in clumps.

I looked over to confirm my suspicions. There they were, two more of them, dressed in minidresses and bejeweled flip-flops, the other California uniform for all seasons. They were all drinking (shudder) giant bottles of kombucha, a drink actually made to taste exactly like vinegar that people drink because they think vinegar is good for you.

"Oh my *God*," High Bun droned as she plopped down next to her friends, "It took me, like, eight hours to find this place! *Whatever!*"

"Oh my *God*, I know," her friend Ponytail drawled. "This town is, like, so backward. It's like 'Hi, it's called legible street signs. Get a *clue.*'"

"Oh my *God*, I know," a girl with her hair in two long braids—Braids—groaned.

They were like a bubble gum–snapping, flip-flopping three-headed monster. As soon as the game started, they whipped out their phones and started scrolling through whatever girls like that scroll through on their phones. Probably pictures of each other.

High Bun held out her phone and smiled at it.

*CLICK!*

What kind of person keeps that sound on their phone?

The same person who starts off a soccer game taking a picture of herself.

*CLICK! CLICK!*

"Which one is your sister?" Braids asked.

"She's number sixty-two. She's all, like, forward. Like offense," Ponytail explained.

"Oh my *God*, she's so cute," Braids squealed.

"She's, like, the only person playing today who doesn't need braces and plastic surgery. She's totally cute." High Bun squinted and aimed her phone at the field.

*CLICK!*

"Crows versus *dogs*," Braids cackled.

"Look at this!" High Bun passed her phone to Ponytail. "It's like 'Hi, I don't care about my overbite.'"

On the field, a skirmish broke out as a bunch of kids lunged for the ball and landed in a pile. I pictured the three-headed monster on the field, at the bottom of the pile, me on the top, my cleats—

Braids yawned. "This team sucks."

"I think a couple of these kids are, like, Mexican. They're probably not even legal," High Bun added, thumbing through her photos.

I fumed, my vision blurring so their little stupid heads were swimming in soupy sunlight. I tried to focus on my hands pressed into my lap.

"That girl needs an eating disorder," one of them said.

They all thought that was hysterical.

*Focus on Tesla*, I thought. I watched as she ran onto the field to play defense.

"I am a good sister," I whispered. "I am a good sister."

At halftime, with the score tied 1–1, I headed down to the field to wish Tesla good luck and prove to my moms that I was, you know, there.

Momma Jo was retying Tesla's laces. "Those kids are

gigantic," she marveled as she patted Tesla's shoes. "You just stay out of their way."

"I'll crush them," Tesla growled, slamming her fist into her open palm with a loud *smack*. Then she bounded onto the field to warm up.

"Hey," I said. "Uh. Good game, I'm assuming."

"Hey." Mama Kate appeared with a water bottle and a watermelon slice. "It is! Are you enjoying yourself?"

"Sure."

"Okay, well"—Mama Kate waved with her slice—"we'll see you after."

Momma Jo stood and grabbed the watermelon slice. Which resulted in one of their patented kissy fights.

Mama Kate can actually squeal like a girl when they're having a kissy fight. "Get your own slice!"

Grabbing Mama Kate in a bear hug, Momma Jo waggled her eyebrows. "Gimme a smooch!"

I was in the process of controlling an eye roll when I heard a sharp, almost canine squeak from behind me.

And a *CLICK!*

There was a rustle and a series of squeaky cries of disdain. "Oh my God, *ew*!"

"Oh my God, look, you can see their tongues!"

I whipped around. It was the girls from the bleachers, all three hairstyles, standing a few steps away, staring at High Bun's phone.

One of them burst into hysterics. "Gross!"

Braids grabbed her stomach. "Barf!"

"Let's get out of here before they, like, rape us," High Bun cried, shoving Ponytail toward the bleachers.

I turned back. Momma Jo was happily munching on watermelon and checking her phone. Mama Kate was taking a picture of Tesla on the field.

They hadn't heard.

I jumped over to the left, away from the hair trio, and waved my arms at my moms to get their attention. *"Hey! Okay!* See you after," I yelled.

"Uh. Yes. Bye," Mama Kate said, frowning. "You okay?"

*"Yup!"* I called as I backed my way toward the stands.

*Tweet! Game on!*

By the time I made it to my seat, the game had hit fever pitch, and the crowd swelled. The three-headed girl clump was back in their seats, too. They were all taking pictures of the players with their phones. I shifted over so I was practically sitting on the edge of the bench, putting as much distance between us as possible.

*Just ignore them, just ignore them, just ignore them.*

*CLICK!*

"Does this girl with the pink bow in her hair look retarded to you?" High Bun mused, flashing her phone to Ponytail.

*"Oh my God,* you're such a bitch! *Ha!"*

"I *know.* I'm such a bitch."

"She does look retarded, though. Like, in the chin."

High Bun rolled her eyes and cackled. "I'm posting the

retard's picture to Facebook," she added, taking aim. "Let's see what everyone else thinks."

*Please just shut up and watch the game,* I seethed. Bit my bottom lip.

*You're here to support Tesla. You're here to support Tesla.*

I could feel the velocity of my pulse pushing against my neck, like some frenzied animal trying to escape.

"Okay," High Bun said, holding out her phone to Braids. "My post has three 'Likes' already. So clearly this girl *is* retarded."

Braids grinned. "You're such a bitch!"

"Hey, where's the girl with the fatty lesbians?" High Bun asked. "The humpback whales?"

"Oh my *God*," Braids squeaked. "Look, she's like sitting right next to us!"

Three sets of eyes clicked in my direction. Three heads leaned forward to look at me looking at them.

"Um. Can we help you?" Braids sneered.

"No," I said.

High Bun swiveled slightly. "Um. Stop staring at us, then?"

The beast with many heads laughed.

"She wants to make out with you," Braids said.

"*Ugh!* Lesbians!" High Bun moaned.

I was about to say something when Braids pointed at the field and shrieked.

"Oh my *God*! It's your sister!"

Ponytail jumped to her feet.

Number 62 had the ball and a break. She was taller than

the others by at least a foot, and she was running. Fast. With huge strides, she kicked the ball up the field. Leaving everyone else behind. I watched Tesla crouch. Look at the crowd. Look down the field.

That was when I felt something. An inexplicable nudge. I turned my head to see High Bun, her phone held out toward me. She smiled, clearly about to take my picture.

*Hey, where's the girl with the fatty lesbians?*

The rest of the crowd leaned forward. Screaming. Cheering.

*CLICK!*

High Bun held the phone up higher. Then, as the crowd roared again, her eyes flickered upward and caught my stare.

I could feel my hands trembling. My heart beating like it was a tiny alien fighting to free itself from inside my chest. The sound of my breathing mixed with the noise of the crowd sloshed inside my ears.

High Bun squinted.

*You want to post me to your stupid Facebook page,* I wanted to scream. *I don't think so.*

I reached up to my neck and wrapped my fingers around the stone.

The edges felt good against my fingertips.

Sharp.

*Forget melting. Forget healing touch. If I had a superpower,* I thought, *it would be to obliterate people like you.*

High Bun scowled. She lowered her phone, stood up, and walked past the other girls, presumably so she could sit as far from me as possible.

And then, just as she was about to sit back down, there was a metallic squeak. And the bench we were all sitting on shuddered. A tremor?

I looked around the stands. No one else seemed to notice. People were clapping and stomping their feet.

I looked back, and High Bun was gone.

*"Oh my God, Jennifer!"* Braids and Ponytail jumped up and screamed in unison.

A tall man in a ball cap sitting in front of us turned around as the rest of the stands continued to shout and cheer.

Braids and Ponytail grabbed at their faces. *"Oh my God! Help!"* Braids cried. *"Our friend fell! Help!"*

Ponytail leaned over the railing. *"Jennifer, are you okay?"* she screamed.

A crowd of people around us stopped cheering and looked over the railing. The tall man in the ball cap started racing down the stands. Someone pulled out her phone.

"Call nine-one-one!" someone shouted.

I didn't know what to do. I picked up my bag and ran down the bleachers to the stairs to the edge of the field.

A few minutes later, whistle blows filled the air, mixing with cheers.

"Cubs win!"

The crowd flooded out of the stands.

"Cubs win!"

*Hooray.*

I dizzily wandered through the flood of people to meet my moms in the parking lot. My heart pounding.

*What just happened?*

*"Monty!"* Tesla was pink and sweaty, her chin slick with whatever she'd been chugging that smelled like cherries.

Tesla ran over.

"We *won*," she screamed, grabbing my hand and pumping it vigorously.

"You did great," I said, allowing myself to be jostled. "You played great. You're a soccer wunderkind."

*"Now I get cake!"* Tesla started marching, pumping her fist in the air. *"I get cake! I get cake! Because we won! Because we won!"*

On our way to the car in the parking lot, we passed the girls from the bleachers sitting on the curb. And there she was—High Bun. Braids had her arm around her.

As I passed, High Bun looked up. She was shaking a bit and her face was all puffy. Her leg was covered in blue ice packs. Like sandbags stacked up to prevent a flood.

I had this sudden flash of her ankle underneath. Maybe it was broken. It was probably all bent under those ice packs.

*How did she fall?* I thought. She was just there and then . . .

A few feet over, a woman dressed in a fluffy pink fleece and green pants said something about the stands not being well built.

"A safety hazard," the woman next to her said. "Definitely."

"Girl could have been killed," another fleeced woman agreed.

Tesla skipped forward into my view. "Did you see me defend goal?" she chirped.

"Yeah," I stammered.

"Those stupid Crows." Tesla clenched her hands into fists. "We *crushed them*."

"*Hey!*" Momma Jo waved from the car. "Hurry up! It's time for ice cream! Let's go!"

Broken ankle or not. *Dogs* won. It was time to celebrate.

\* \* \*

The victory party was epic.

Apparently it was our turn to host the post-game party. Girls arrived by the truckloads, the taste of victory still on their strawberry-balmed lips. They gorged on pizza, cake and ice cream, or organic fruit salad with agave syrup, if that was how the kids wanted to roll.

I'm pretty sure they all ate cake. From my room, I could hear them screaming and thumping around in that lots-of-sugar way. Kids my sister's age are the noisiest things on earth. It's hard to believe they're really small and helpless when they can shriek and make your eardrums bleed.

At some point, full of sugar, someone cranked the music to twenty and cried, "Let's *dance!*"

Upstairs, locked in my room, I fell onto my bed and gathered my couch cushions around me. I felt jittery, like someone who hasn't had enough or has had too much coffee. Everything in my room seemed loud. Even the walls were loud. The night outside was loud.

I wanted to call Naoki or Thomas, but I had no idea what I would say.

*What happened?*

I was at the game, these girls were being crappy and mean, and then . . .

Then what? Did I do something? Did I somehow push her off the bleachers?

I touched the stone around my neck.

There was a knock on the door. Momma Jo's muffled voice. "You hungry?"

"Uh, yeah. I mean, come in."

There was a pause. "You wanna open the door since I'm bringing you food?"

"Oh." I jumped off the bed and opened the door.

Momma Jo stood in the hallway with a tray of victory snacks: a mini sundae with chocolate sauce and graham crackers, and some corn chips and salsa and real guacamole on the side. Momma makes guacamole with extra mayo the way I like it, with huge chunks of avocado in it so it's like cookies-and-cream ice cream but with avocado.

With the door open, the music was deafening. "Holy cow," I said, stepping back to let her in the room and shutting the door resolutely behind her. "Are they having a rave or something?"

"Or something," Momma Jo grumbled, placing the tray on the bed. "There's more cake down . . . Hey," she said, picking up her foot. Underneath was a pile of my most recent scavenges of balled-up Reverend White posters.

"What's this?" She kicked the Reverend White's face, un-crinkled, with her sandal.

"Oh," I said, sitting back down on the bed. "It's just a stu-pid poster."

"Looks like a few stupid posters." Momma Jo bent down and picked up a crumpled poster. She stared at the Reverend White. Then scowled. "Well, just because this is California doesn't mean there's no assholes allowed."

Secretly—that is, not in earshot of Mama Kate—Momma Jo has a pretty solid opinion that people like the Reverend White are assholes. They bug her the way actual bugs bug her. She doesn't like them, and she doesn't want them in her house.

When I was little, when girls were always making me cry, I would picture Momma Jo saying "assholes."

Sometimes it helped if I was wearing her sweatshirt when I thought it. *Assholes.*

Momma Jo tucked her hair behind her ears and sat down on the only corner of the bed not taken up by cushions, laundry, or snacks. Then she gave me the face she gives when she is about to talk to me about something and she wants me to know she is serious. It involves a very crinkled forehead and a frown.

I shrugged. "Not a big deal."

Momma Jo sat back. Looked at me for a bit. Then she reached over to the tray and broke off a piece of chip. "It's not? I mean, you know, it could be . . . hard," she said, dipping the chip in the guacamole. "Even if you know that our family doesn't need to be saved by the Reverend White."

"I know," I said, crawling back into my couch-cushion nest.

"You know," Momma Jo added, grabbing another chip, "your Mama Kate is pretty much constantly worrying about how you are, so I feel I should also ask how you are doing."

"Everything's fine," I said, reaching over and grabbing a

chip and a scoop of guacamole. "She should stop worrying. Tell her to stop worrying."

Momma Jo threw up her hands. "Well, that's your Mama Kate. She does that worrying thing."

"Everything's okay." I grabbed a chip and dunked it to my fingertips in guacamole. "Promise."

Momma Jo paused. Looked at me for what felt like two minutes. Like time-out long. "Okay. Let me know if it's too loud down there. I think your sister and her friends want to watch *America's Next Top Model* if you want to join us."

I shoved the whole chip into my mouth. "Pass," I said through the chip.

"Fair enough," Momma Jo said. "I'll shut the door behind me."

I gobbled down the rest of my treats. Then I pulled the stone off my neck. And looked at it.

I flipped it over in my palm.

The Eye of Know.

What did I know? Did I see the future or the past? With my third eye?

No.

No, I saw what I always saw, girls being mean for no reason.

But this time. Maybe this time, instead of just watching it happen, I made something happen. I made her stop. I made it go away.

Didn't I?

"Maybe I did, maybe it was something else," I said. My voice sounded weird in my quiet room.

"It could have been an earthquake," I said to my blank computer screen.

Either way.

No more selfies.

The stone swung back and forth on its string. What would I tell Thomas and Naoki?

Thomas wouldn't believe me, although this did feel more like a movie plot than anything else I had ever found.

A stone that could make things happen.

Monty's Stone.

Why not? Just because someone doesn't think something is possible, whether that's bending time or seeing the future, doesn't mean it's not.

*What's impossible?* Impossible *sounds like a Madison Marlow word*, I thought.

I could see her clicking her nails on the desk. *Tick, tick, tick.* Rolling her eyes at me. "That's *impossible*, Monty." Like "*Everyone knows, duh.*"

*Well*, I wanted to crow, *guess what?*

The Eye of Know was possible. Inexplicable but REAL. An unexplained phenomenon I could actually hold in my hand. I had seen that girl practically disappear in front of my eyes.

Hadn't I?

The world was bigger than Aunty, California. There were more possibilities out there than anyone at Jefferson, especially Madison and her crew, could guess.

It made me feel light just thinking about it.

I needed to talk to Naoki, I thought.

Naoki would get it.

I grabbed my phone from my bag.

No texts.

It was late, so she'd probably be on her computer.

Me: Hey you there?
Me: Hello?

Minutes ticked by.

I put the Eye on my bedside table.

Below me, the party raged.

A well-deserved victory party, maybe for all of us.

# 7

☺ Mystics

☺ Table-tipping (See also: Séance)

☹ Why people put statues of angels on their lawn

OVER THE WEEKEND, TESLA HAD SOCCER GAMES
back-to-back, so I had the house to myself. I spent my freedom
watching online documentaries about American mystics and
people who can talk to the dead.

One mystic used little plastic dolls to communicate with
the spirits. Like the kind of dolls I would imagine grand-
mas collecting. With little painted faces and frozen china
hands.

The dead are very forgiving and are never sad about being

dead. Apparently that's something built into the system so that no one feels ripped off in the afterlife.

A couple of the mystics talked about Jesus a lot. About how Jesus was at work in the world of the living and the dead, shepherding people into heaven. Like Jesus was some kind of maître d' for heaven. *If he's so important*, I wondered, *why is he working the door?*

These people have no logic.

There was this part in one documentary where all the mystics put their hands on the table and it danced around. It's called table-tipping.

*Interesting*, I thought.

At one point, on my way to grab a slice at Tony's Pizza Pie around the block, I took the stone out to a crosswalk to see if I could affect when the lights changed, which is something this guy I found online said he could do with just his brain (which is part alien). Hard to say if it was working; people kept pressing the buttons, so it could have been them.

Naoki spent the weekend at a weaving seminar, sending me pictures every so often of layers of pink and blue and yellow threads. Thomas spent the weekend binge watching eighties romantic comedies, which apparently he can only do alone.

By Monday, I was kind of sick of just being by myself.

That morning, I came downstairs, and Tesla was sitting at the breakfast table in a sparkly pink leotard and tutu, next to a bowl of what looked like black spiderwebs.

I thumped down on my seat and pushed the bowl with my finger. "What's that?"

"*Don't*," Tesla huffed. "It's my hair stuff. Mama's putting my hair up in a fairy bun."

I had a flash of High Bun, her phone held out.

*CLICK.*

"Why a bun?"

"Because it's Halloween? Duh? And I'm a fairy."

*Halloween?* I poured myself a giant bowl of cereal and scanned the table for sugar. *How did Halloween sneak up on me? Weird.*

I looked over at Tesla, suddenly noticing that her hair was already sprayed and pinned into place. "Fairies have buns?"

Also weird:

☹ Kids' obsession with fairies

To be clear, every year, for Halloween, Tesla dresses up as a fairy, which, every year, involves some specific fairy thing that I've never heard of. When she was eight, it meant she had to have ballet slippers. Last year, when she was ten, she asked to be a "sexy fairy," and my parents asked her to explain what a sexy fairy would look like.

She drew a picture.

Sexy fairy had a bra over her outfit.

"No sexy fairy," Momma Jo said. "You're a ten-year-old fairy. A ten-year-old fairy doesn't need a bra."

Neither does an eleven-year-old fairy, apparently.

Every year since this fairy stuff started I take the opportunity to explain to her what fairies were really like, and it bugs the crap out of her.

I leaned over my bowl and pointed at Tesla with my spoon. "Did I ever tell you that fairies actually looked ugly and mean?"

Tesla crossed her arms over her fairy chest. "No, they weren't."

"Some people thought they were an omen of death!"

"Shut up, Monty."

Unperturbed, I munched on my cereal. "Are you an omen of death, Tesla?"

It's true they were. Not always, but sometimes. Fairies, in the original stories about fairies, weren't these wishy-washy, wistful wish granters in tutus, like they are in kids' books today. They were mean, vengeful. Sometimes because they were cast out of their villages, sent to the woods without supper. In the first stories about fairies, they used their magic to disguise themselves. To do bad things. They were mess-you-uppers, enchanters.

☺ Omens
☺ Enchantments

And by *enchant*, we're not talking about a sprinkle of fairy dust so you can fly. We're talking *you will obey me*-type stuff. *Give me your wife*-type stuff.

There is actually a support group in Daytona for people who have been attacked by fairies. It has a very grim website.

It also has a 1-800 number, which I have often considered calling.

It's funny, though, right, that a word like *enchanting* sounds so nice, like a really nice afternoon, like something special, but really, it's also a spell.

A trick.

None of which Tesla wanted to hear as Mama Kate continued to pin her hair into the toughest bun in California, but I made a mental note to mention it to Naoki because it sounded like a Naoki sort of thing. Enchanted.

In the car on the way to school I got a text from Naoki.

Naoki: Old Man Tree lunch OK?
Me: Working on Outsiders deco with T. After school?
Naoki: Just need a minute. OM at 12:30?

Thomas came to school in drag, which he takes the Halloween option to do sometimes. Over the years, Thomas has shown a preference for queens: Queen Elizabeth II, the Queen of Hearts. This Halloween he was the evil queen from Snow White, in a purple dress and cape, a black wig, a crown I think he actually welded himself, and a big, real red apple, which he would hold up when people wanted to take pictures.

Queen or not, from the moment the lunch bell rang, Thomas was full-tilt working on sets, his skirts hitched up, an old-timey-looking apron tied around his waist, and a paintbrush in each hand as he slaved to make a realistic movable set of trees and classic cars for the upcoming production of *The Outsiders.* Mr. Gyle, true to his word, had hired a "choreographer" to help students with the fight scenes. Of which there were many. The choreographer showed up in a Raiders sweatshirt, hat, and jogging pants. He wore bright green sneakers. He looked like a football coach. And talked like a football coach.

I'm pretty sure he was a football coach.

Thomas said he overheard him saying stuff like "Hut hut hut" instead of, say, "Action."

I was a few minutes into my volunteered lunch hour spent sitting in a plastic chair with a metal brush and sewing scissors, distressing jeans for the "actors," before Thomas told me who I was distressing for.

The actor taking the lead role in Hinton's formidable tale of adolescent struggle? MATT TRUIT.

"What?!" "When did they post it?"

"Friday," Thomas said, stirring a can of classic-car crimson. "He was really the best of the bunch."

*"Are you serious?!"*

Matt Truit? Really? How much injustice should one person have to endure?

How is it possible that someone who makes a sport of *making fun* of something then gets to *benefit from its existence*?

I'd heard a rumor in the girls' bathroom that Kenneth White had auditioned, too, but Thomas said it wasn't true. He said Kenneth showed up and sat in the back of the theater, but then, when they tried to talk to him, he just left.

"What's worse?" I sighed, tossing my newly—*Matt's* newly—distressed jeans on the floor.

"It's not so bad," Thomas said, bending over to pick them up.

"*Pfft* is all I have to say to that."

"While you're *pfft*ing you can put these on a hanger and onto the costume rack, please," Thomas said, holding out the pants.

"*Fine.* I bet Kenneth didn't audition because it's such a disgusting, sinful play," I chortled. "Poor Kenneth with all this sin everywhere."

I hung up Matt's pants and grabbed the undistressed pair next in line. It was harder to do now that I knew I was distressing jeans for jerkoffs.

Thomas turned back to his can of crimson. "He looks a little like the older-brother character to me."

How was it Thomas could stay so relaxed around people being crazy homophobes all the time? He dipped his brush into the new bucket of paint and brushed a stroke onto the door of a massive wooden car.

I tore into my new set of pants with the iron brush. "Did I tell you he corrected me in chemistry today?"

Thomas didn't look up. "Matt?"

"Kenneth."

Basically, I was in chemistry and I'd said something about hydrogen in class, and Kenneth had chuckled.

Chuckled. Actually jiggled in his seat. Like, he went from nothing to chuckle. It wasn't even that funny.

He didn't turn around. He'd just said, "I'm pretty sure you mean oxygen."

"Okay, well, in other news, the play is cast—hurrah," Thomas said, moving from the car to the stack of trees in the corner of the room. "You know, now that I've had a closer look, Matt's not a bad-looking guy. I can see what you saw in him."

I looked down at the jeans. I'd been scrubbing them so hard I'd almost torn them in half. "Whatever. I've got to go. I told Naoki I'd meet her by the Old Man."

"Don't forget your cat ears," Thomas called, pointing at my fuzzy ears with his free hand as he dragged a stack of trees onto the stage.

As I wandered outside to the courtyard in front of the school I noted that I was one of about twenty cats, a cat being the go-to minimalist costume choice. Only about half the kids at school had bothered to dress up. By the time you get to high school, no one's really trick-or-treating, so it's mostly a matter of who *actually* likes to dress up for their own interest. Mostly it's nerds, who will take on any excuse to dress up like their favorite action heroes or creatures.

There were a lot of Gandalfs wandering around.

☹ Boys' obsession with wizards

There are four trees in the quad next to Jefferson High. One looks like a spaceship hovering on top of a pencil, which is where the teachers sit when they have lunch. One looks like an Afro, which is where people usually go to make out because it's the most tucked to the side. There's the super big pointy-at-the-top tree that popular people eat lunch under because it's supposedly the nicest. And there's Old Man tree, all bent over and crooked and knobbly, where the nerds eat because it's closest to the school and the Wi-Fi signal they hack into is better there, even though the ground is a little rockier.

Naoki was waiting for me under the tree, dressed in blue and gray and green, with little bits of things pinned to her. Leaves. Twigs. Moss.

"I'm a river," she explained.

"Cool." Of course, because I had like a zillion things I wanted to tell Naoki, about the Eye, the incantation, about Tesla's soccer game, I was suddenly struck completely dumb. Wasn't there a word I was going to ask her about? "Cool," I said again for no reason.

Naoki smiled. "Okay, good," she said, as though I'd just said something that could be described as "good." "So, I have a question to ask you," she continued, "about Mystery Club. And our membership. I want to suggest a new member."

"Who?"

"He's new. And I haven't asked him, but I think we should," Naoki added.

"Okaaay."

There was a shriek on the other side of the school. The sun poured down between the branches and set a warm spot on the top of my head.

Naoki grabbed a lock of hair, twisted it artfully into a loop.

"Okay, so first I'm going to say it, then I'm going to explain. Okay. I think we should ask Kenneth White to join Mystery Club."

"What?!"

The crowd of nerds, gathered several feet away for a few impromptu rounds of Magic, cringed.

Naoki put her hands out, palms up, like an offering. "Right, so I'll explain. Remember last week, with the crosses? Of course you remember. Okay, on that day, I started thinking about the word *cross*. About being 'cross' as in 'angry,' about the shape of a cross, and crossing paths. I thought about it all night. *Cross. Cross. Cross.* And the next day, I started crossing paths with Kenneth. Over and over. Our paths would literally cross, you know? Me coming from the north and him from the west."

"Yeah."

*Like the Wicked Witch.*

"Sooooo," I said slowly, "what are you saying, then?"

Naoki sped up. "Okay. So I thought, *Why is this happening? What is it about the word* cross? *Or about Kenneth?* I thought of the time I found you and Thomas." Naoki started tracing out a path in the air with her index finger. "I was in the library. Waiting for a book to find me. And you were in your study hall, talking about mysteries. And I'd been thinking about being lost. And the mystery of lost. How lost is a mystery. And I just thought, you know, that maybe there is no book with what I'm looking for. The word *book* felt so far away. And I was walking down the hall and I heard you say 'mystery,' and I thought how life can be a perfect mystery. And then I found you."

Her index finger pointed at me. Naoki smiled.

"Okaaaaay." I could feel the little stones on the ground digging into my feet.

"I think what all this cross and crossing paths means is that Kenneth is supposed to be in our cross paths." Naoki took a deep breath. "That's it."

"I don't get it." I could feel myself coiling inward. "Uh," I stammered, "just so we're clear, this is the guy who glued a cross to my locker."

Which I still had in my bag, incidentally.

The gravelly rhythm of sneakers grinding against dirt roused in the distance. Naoki's face stayed still, soft but frozen like a snowman's. "Are you sure it was him?"

"Uh. No, if by 'sure' you mean I saw him do it."

Naoki tapped her finger on her lip. Her nails were painted green and blue. "Hmmmm. I don't think it was him."

"Puh!" I scoffed. "Why not?"

"I just, I don't see it. I can't explain it. I just feel this overwhelming thing, like we are supposed to cross paths."

"Well, maybe you're supposed to cross paths with him separately." I could feel my words speeding up, running hotter and hotter.

Naoki paused. Tapped her lip again. "I mean we, like, all of us."

"Well, I don't want to have to hang out with a homophobe."

"Maybe he isn't."

"Maybe it's less of a big deal for you if he is," I spat.

Naoki shifted and crossed one foot over the other. Waiting. Maybe for me to say something else. I don't know what.

"Hmmmmm," she said finally. "Could we say we're going to think about it?"

It was pointless to say no. I mean, technically, it was my and Thomas's club more than it was Naoki's. And technically Naoki had no business even really thinking about who should be a member. But it seemed mean to point that out.

In the ground I noticed a sharp rock sticking up out of the dirt. I kicked it lightly with the toe of my boot. There is an art to dislodging rocks like this. You have to wiggle them very gently until they come loose like a tooth.

"Monty?" Naoki tilted her head.

The rock wasn't budging. I gave it another kick.

*Hey, guess what,* I thought. It was also true that, for a really nice person, Naoki was actually acting like kind of a homophobe. I'm sure, I thought, she would never think that. Even though it was true.

I could feel my brain filling up with angry bits, piling up like Ho Ho wrappers on a binge day. Like homework on a Sunday.

Naoki stared at me. I stared at my unmoving rock.

"Okay, well . . ." is all I got past my lips.

"Okay, well. Let's just see," Naoki said, her voice a whisper in the breeze.

"Sure." I gave the rock one more kick.

"Okay. Amazing." Naoki started to turn back to the school. "Hey, so what's up with the Eye of Know?"

"Uh." I looked down. Picked some stray threads off the leg of my jeans. "Maybe later."

"Maybe later." Naoki shrugged. "Bye."

And she gathered up her stuff and waved goodbye. Coincidentally, the sun tucked itself away into a little gray cloud, which decided to take up residence over my head.

On my way to class, I spotted him, Mr. Kenneth White. Not in costume. Unless he was dressed up as someone who wore the same son-of-an-evangelical-preacher non-outfit of denim and white every day. He was looking out the window, his arms crossed.

I had this thought where I would go up to him and say, "I've seen your dad's videos, you know."

I had. On Friday night, as Tesla celebrated, while I waited for Naoki to IM me back, I'd sat and watched a bunch of his dad's videos.

There were a lot of them.

"I saw a video of you and your dad in New York," I would say, "when you were protesting a wedding. It was a video taken by someone who was supposed to be filming the wedding of a friend or something. And the lesbians getting married are in white, and they're standing in a park with their friends and family. Just some little park with ducks and stuff. And one of the lesbians is wearing a suit and the other is wearing this big dress. And the video goes in and out of focus. And all of a sudden, your dad walks in with a bullhorn, screaming about saving the American family. And the last thing the camera

zooms in on is his stupid face. In his stupid white suit. At someone else's wedding."

Maybe he would look at me. Then I'd get to say, "And there
is no way you're going to be a member of the only other group
outside my family that I care about in this world."

*That's what I should say*, I thought.

*Not that you would hear it.*

*Even though it's true.*

Suddenly I thought of the Eye. I flipped my bag off my back
and started digging inside for it.

But then Kenneth looked up and started walking, and it oc-
curred to me that we were about to cross paths, so I picked up
my bag and scooted back and around the other side of the
building.

See, it is possible to avoid a prophecy, I thought. It just de-
pends on where you step.

It was still a few minutes to bell, so I headed to my locker,
bumping into Thomas, in full Queen.

"Going to your locker?" he asked in sing-song.

"Yeah."

"How's Naoki?" he asked in regular voice.

"Fine."

"Okay." Thomas raised an eyebrow. "Hey, I thought you said
you were going to be the Joker for Halloween."

"Yeah, I forgot."

Next to my locker a crew of Jefferson's most popular stood
comparing costumes.

Madison Marlow had come as Hillary Clinton, which impressed most of the teachers. I didn't think she looked all that much like Hillary Clinton except that she was wearing kind of a business-suit-type outfit. It looked a little slutty to be Hillary. I don't think Hillary wears a lot of miniskirts.

About a dozen other girls were dressed up in . . . basically what looked like underwear to me.

Sixteen-year-old fairy time.

I looked over to catch Thomas giving an appraising look.

"Your drag is way better than theirs," I whispered, opening my locker.

"The Kardashians stuffed their butts," Thomas whispered back, pointing at the Parte twins.

"With real butt stuffing," I sneered.

I was about to close my locker when I was hit with a heavy thud against my back. *"What are you supposed to be? A black hole?"*

*"Hey!"* I spun around.

*"Oooohh.* Testy!" It was Matt. Wearing what looked like a weird mix of a Walmart ninety-nine-cent witch costume and a pound of horror makeup. He leaned against the row of lockers. "How do I look? I know you gays are the fashion committee around here, so I thought I'd ask. Do I look like a leading man?"

"MATT!"

Matt threw his hands in the air. "Hey, man, relax! Okay? I'm getting into character. Ready for my big debut."

"Go away." I stepped back. Out of the corner of my eye, I could see the twinkle of Thomas's crown as he hovered.

"You don't like my outfit? Maybe I just need a prop. Excuse me, Propmaster." Matt spun around, snatching Thomas's apple from his hand.

"Hey! Give that back!" That was me, not Thomas, by the way. Thomas just rolled his eyes.

Matt tossed the apple in the air, caught it, and walked off down the hallway.

"Did he really just steal your apple?" I screeched.

Thomas brushed the wig hair out of his eyes. "It's just an apple. I've got fifteen cents to get another one."

"It's not about fifteen cents, Thomas!"

*I am standing in a hailstorm, and I'm the only one who can see it's raining,* my brain screamed. It cooked with the thought till my eyes watered.

Thomas looked at me. His lips were painted cherry red, outlined so they curled up. So it was an effort to frown. Which he was, just a little. "I know it's not. But it's *still* only fifteen cents," Thomas said, adjusting his crown. "Cue bell."

☹ Why Thomas puts up with everything and doesn't get mad

That day, instead of study hall, we had Intramural Sports Day.

So everyone had to do an intramural sport.

Mandatory physical fitness. GOOD FOR US ALL, read the poster decorated with stock photos of smiling kids.

For whatever reason, I'd signed up for soccer.

Some of the kids showed up on the field in their costumes. One kid just changed out his pants so he was an intergalactic warrior in track pants. A girl named Susie insisted on wearing her bunny ears.

I threw on the only sports gear I had, which was an old pair of track pants and one of Momma Jo's field hockey jerseys. I took a very, very, very wide, and de facto defensive, position.

Which is to say I walked to the edge of the field and lay down on the grass, hoping not to be noticed.

### ☹ Matt Truit

Matt Truit.

There are so many reasons not to like Matt Truit.

It is not even worth counting.

He is obnoxious.

He is mean.

He is a jerk.

The worst thing about Matt Truit, the worst thing of all, is the fact that I didn't always hate Matt Truit.

The word I was looking for earlier popped into my head. Like a beacon or a crooked cartoon halo.

*Enchanting*.

### ☹ Enchanting Jerks and ME

Right.

For seventy-two hours, his first seventy-two hours in Aunty, when he transferred last year, I actually liked Matt Truit.

Maybe even a lot.

I remember what he looked like that first day. I can actually see him standing at the front of the class. From Ohio, the teacher had said. Matt's one foot was kind of shaking a bit, but he had this big smile on his big lips. And he was wearing a T-shirt that said HUG ME on it.

Mr. Todd told him to sit next to me, and I was supposed to, like, show him around. Thomas and Naoki were both out sick, so I was kind of like, you know, "Hey, why not?"

And so there was Matt Truit plopped down next to me. Smelling like soap.

"Nice shirt," I said.

And Matt smiled and he said, "Are you the official fashion police?"

It wasn't a mean or shitty statement back then. It was just, like, a joke.

And I said, "There's not really a police so much as a Committee of Appropriate School Wear, of which I am a member."

Anyway. He drew this weird little potato man on my math book for me. This angry potato that could cook himself and then eat himself.

It was really funny.

For lunch, he took me out to McDonald's to thank me for helping him, which was kind of cool because, you know, it wasn't like I was tutoring him or anything. I'd been asked to sit with him in a class.

While we waited in line, he did all these impressions of all these dopey kids from Ohio. And he said California was full of hippies, which it is.

I did my impression of this art teacher we used to have who used to praise everyone's work with this deep "*whoooa,*" which always sounded like "*duuuude*" to me.

"*Whoooa. Look at your painting, Montgomery. It's like . . . whoooa.*"

After we got our food, I didn't know where to sit or whether to sit. All the tables were full of Madison Marlows and their posses. So I just stood there, holding my tray like a dork, until Matt stepped ahead of me and walked over to a booth.

"You just gonna stand there?"

Halfway through his burger, Matt looked up and pointed at me with a fry. "You have really cute lips," he said, then popped the fry in his mouth. "Like, they're a cupid's bow. That's a thing, right?"

"Oh yeah?" My hands shook a little as I tried to casually sip on my soda and not choke on my straw.

"Yeah." Matt looked down at his burger, smiling. "They're really cute. They're like a painting or something. You have a boyfriend?"

My body forgot how to stop drinking from a straw. I had to literally lift my head off it. Like a crazy person. "Uh. No."

Matt didn't seem to notice. "You should. You're too cute to be single. You a virgin?"

A little chill ran up my arms. "What?"

"It's a joke. You should wear skirts. I bet you've got nice legs."

Why hadn't I seen it?

Because I'm an idiot.

The next morning in math, he carved all this stuff into my textbook, then he kind of ran off after class. Then, in the afternoon, he ran into me in the hallway and asked me to come help him with his math homework at lunch the next day.

"After you carved up my textbook?" I said, standing in the hallway, wearing the only short skirt I owned (a garage sale find).

Matt stared at my legs, then looked up at me and smiled a huge celebrity smile. "What? That was art! That was me giving my art to you! You should be grateful."

I said yes. *Yes, I will help you.*

Because I'm stupid.

"Nice skirt."

We sat on a hill by the soccer field, his notebook half on his lap and half on mine. He slid his hand under the flap, up onto my thigh. His hand brushed over my skin, over my fuzzy legs that I hadn't shaved because I almost never thought about my legs as something someone would see or touch.

My body quaked a bit. I started to shift away.

"You know what? I bet you want to kiss me," he said. And he smiled. A new smile I didn't know yet.

I could feel the skin on my thigh getting warm under his touch. "Oh yeah?"

"Yeah, I'm pretty sure you do."

I leaned forward and I kissed him. He basically asked me to. And I wanted to because at the time I thought he was cute.

I thought he liked me. I thought, you know, he's funny. He's not like the kids here. He's different.

I was enchanted. We had three soft kisses. They were these amazing little melty kisses.

Then his hand grabbed my thigh. Clamped down. And all the sudden it was just like *tongue*. And I pulled back.

"Relax." He smiled, and he pulled me on top of his lap. I remember the pencil in my pocket jabbing into my side as I crawled on top of him and shoved the textbook aside. And I felt—okay, yeah, I felt this immediate surge. Like, a want. Like I wanted him.

We kissed again. I learned to manage the overwhelmingness of tongue. And the meltiness came back.

But that feeling was quickly replaced by something else, specifically his hand pushing under the front of my sweater. I could feel him searching for my boobs, like, clawing past my T-shirt in this weird, frustrated way.

"Uh. Wait! Wait. No." I put my hand on his, which was firmly entrenched on the edge of my bra.

"Uh! What?" Matt rolled his eyes.

I started to sweat. "Um. I mean. It's just . . . really public here. I don't want to—"

Matt leaned back. Appraising. "What's wrong with you?"

"Nothing! I just—"

"Oh my God, I knew it." Matt slid out from under me, stood up fast, brushed the grass off the back of his jeans. "You're a dyke, right?"

I sat in the grass, curled my knees up. "No! Wait. What? Why would you ask me that?"

"Forget it."

It was weird, suddenly not knowing what someone knew. Had someone told him about my moms? I mean, I would have said something, I guess. I just hadn't gotten to it yet.

The sun beat down on the top of my head.

"I gotta go," he said. "Later."

And he just walked away.

The next day, Matt didn't sit next to me in math. He sat at the back with these other guys. After class I found him in the hall, and I grabbed Thomas, who was finally back in school, to introduce him to Matt.

As I grabbed Matt's arm, I felt him pull away. And he kind of let out this noise. This, like, scoff.

And I was like, *Oh. Wait.*

Oh wait, this is not what I thought it would be for a teeny-tiny second. Oh wait, it's what I've thought it would be since I got to this crummy school and realized everyone who goes here is an asshole. Oh wait, never mind. Never mind whatever I said to you, I wanted to tell Matt. I "un" this whole week. I take it back.

I *un*-kiss you. I *un*-like you.

I *un*-touch you and *un*-want you to touch me.

Whatever happened now officially *did not happen.*

I remember the three of us just standing there. Thomas, Matt, and me. And Matt kind of looking at me. And smirking.

"Uh. Matt," I said hesitantly, "this is my friend Thomas."

"Charmed." Thomas smiled, holding out his hand for a handshake.

"Uh. Right." Matt turned and looked at his friends. Turned back. Looked at me. Smirked. "Charmed."

A few days after that, he was walking with the football team, like almost the whole team, and I passed him in the hallway. I was a few steps away when I heard, "Just because she's a dyke doesn't mean I'm not gonna tap that."

That's pretty much the whole story.

Except to say that I threw the skirt away.

Except to say that after that, I heard Matt tell Madison Marlow's boyfriend, or boyfriend at the time, Fred Brewer, that I jumped him his first day. And I offered to have sex with him. Because I'm desperate for sex. Even though I'm a dyke. I'm desperate to have man sex.

"Don't listen to them," Thomas always says. "There's nothing they have to say that has any value. So it's not worth listening to."

*Then they should all just shut up*, I thought. But they don't. They just keep talking and saying whatever they want, because who will stop them?

"*Hey!*" someone screamed, and I looked up to see a soccer ball headed my way, kicked ferociously by a Parte twin.

Mrs. MacDonald, phys ed teacher extraordinaire, finally noticed my horizontal position.

"*Get up, Sole!*"

I stood up just in time to spot a girl in a rainbow wig and a My Little Pony T-shirt charging toward me. I ran to the ball, throwing my foot out as it rolled my way. I kicked the ball . . . right into my team's goal.

Game over.

## 8

ON TUESDAY, I WOKE UP, TUMBLING. IN MY DREAM, I was scaling this path around this mountain. Momma Jo and Mama Kate and Tesla were ahead of me.

The bridge was made up of black slats, dark like the Eye. Each step looked like a black hole.

*What if they are black holes?* I thought. My brain was dream-mushy.

I reached around my neck. The Eye wasn't there.

Was it the bridge? Was it safe?

"Wait!" I yelled.

Everyone on the path just turned and looked at me. No one moved.

The bridge shook and Tesla slipped backward, shrieking.

*"Help!"* I screamed.

I woke up, and I was standing on the edge of my bed, still falling backward.

"Montgomery," said a black bird perched on my computer, feathers flapping in the wind. "You're still dreaming."

☺ Dream control and not control

It's called a false awakening. You think you're awake, but you're still in the dream.

"*Agh!*"

Tesla's scream. My default alarm clock.

"*Mommmmaaahhh!*"

I threw on what looked like a relatively clean top and my overalls. Tucking the Eye of Know into my pocket, I ran downstairs and just ate whatever Momma Jo threw on the table in front of me, which unfortunately turned out to be oatmeal, which is the most disgusting breakfast on the face of the earth. Tesla loves it and sprinkles protein powder on hers. And flax seeds. And whatever else she thinks is going to make her faster and stronger than the average kid.

Today it was green omega powder.

"When did you start sprinkling stuff on your food?" I asked between hesitant mouthfuls.

"Uh. Since forever?" Tesla scoffed, her mouth full of what looked like moss.

"I can't believe you like that stuff."

"Well, obviously we like different things," Tesla said as she frowned.

Under the table I could see she was still only wearing one sock.

"Have you ever considered flip-flops? We do live in California."

"Flip-flops are gross."

"True. Wow. We actually agree."

Tesla rolled her eyes and shoveled another mouthful of oatmeal in her mouth. "Magic," she muffled.

Mama Kate walked into the room and froze.

"Monty, honestly! That shirt is *stained*. Go upstairs and put something else on. You look like you're wearing the dirty hamper."

I sniffed the sleeve. It smelled worn and comfortable, a little bit like toast. There was just a tiny stain on the sleeve. "This is fine," I grumbled. It felt cozy. Also, I noted looking down, it was my Bigfoot shirt. You pretty much can't go wrong with Bigfoot.

Maybe Mama Kate agreed. Maybe she was just too tired to argue. Staring at my shirt, she let out this big breath. "Okay, Monty. Just . . . have a good day." She pulled what was clearly a strategically stashed pair of socks out of her pocket and motioned for Tesla. "Finish up. We don't want to be late."

Tesla had an appointment, so I walked to school that day, which meant it was a coffee-on-the-way-to-school day, which is like my little reward to myself. I get a double Dark

Horse blend, and I put honey and cream in it, and it is delicious. Mary's Grounds only has dark blends and all her pastries are full of gluten. And Mary, whose name is Phyllis, doesn't take cards. And she doesn't like talking to people.

So, of course, I am a loyal customer.

I was sipping and walking when I saw them. The latest flood of posters from the Reverend White. On every pole between coffee and school.

## THE REVEREND WHITE WANTS YOU TO SAVE THE AMERICAN FAMILY!

The night before, fueled by my masterful soccer game and fabulous day at school, I'd watched more Reverend White vs. Gay Wedding videos. Now when I looked at the posters, I could hear his voice ringing in my ears, calling out from a crackling megaphone. "It's evil and it's everywhere, brothers and sisters. Not a union of God. Evil."

The posters had changed. No more posters with the happy family being coddled by a loving White. Now it was just him. Magnanimous. Arms wide. Not arms wide like "let me give you a hug." Arms wide like "I am saving you."

I could see him standing behind the pulpit.

Across the street, a woman pushing a stroller with a kid on her hip looked up at the poster. Down the road, a tall man shifted his ball cap as he leaned in to get a closer look. How many people were reading this and thinking, *Yeah, that's what this town needs, someone to take a stand against the freaks who think they can disobey the laws of Adam and Eve and all that biblical stuff that says there's only one way to do the whole family thing?* How many people would join up with the Reverend White?

A truck roared by, fast and loud, country music blaring. It made my heart pound a bit, in this nervous way, like my heart wanted me to be running.

## THE REVEREND WHITE WANTS YOU

I reached up and grabbed the poster, crumpled it into my bag.

By the time I got to school, I was kind of sweaty. I tried to just switch my brain to autopilot, just get through the day. I ran my laps at gym. During lunch, I went to help Thomas paint a bunch of trees for the set. I could hear Matt and the boys rehearsing onstage.

"Okay, guys"—Coach Choreographer clapped his hands—"greasers on this side and the, uh, other guys over here. Matt! Eyes front! What's your name? Yah, you too. Okay, now we're going to fight with just some light slaps, okay? Nothing too hard."

Matt chuckled. "Get Thomas out here to show us some light slaps."

I hadn't realized he could see backstage. I looked up, and there was Matt waving at us through the curtains.

What happened after that? Bio. Surrounded by the

smell of bleach, I tried to think about something that didn't make my head hurt, while, at the front of the class, Mr. Jenner cycled through endless PowerPoint presentations of hearts. Lungs.

After school, I was supposed to meet Thomas on the far side of the field, and we were going to walk to this hardware store to get some supplies for set building.

As I walked out, there were kids selling crafts and snacks for different charities and teams. Which I have always found kind of weird. Like, why do I have to pay fifty cents for a coconut square so the soccer team can have new uniforms? As I thought this, I nearly slammed into the CHEER TREATS FOR BREAST CANCER table, staffed by a bunch of girls in cheerleading uniforms.

They all had the same squeaky, high voices. "Um, can you even be careful?" One of them said, "This is for *breast* cancer."

"Um. Okay," I said. "How much for a treat?"

"Uh. The sign says two dollars."

"Pfft," another girl scoffed. "Obviously."

I noticed all their nails were painted pink. *Little pink claws*, I thought.

"Fine," I said, grabbing a treat and tossing two dollars on the table. "Thanks for the great customer service."

There's something about the way the girls at this school look at me, like I'm some sort of genetic experiment. Like a hairy monster.

I wish I felt like Naoki seems to feel. Like some sort of beautiful mythical creature.

*Screw them.*

Ten minutes later, I was standing in the field and eating my for-breast-cancer Rice Krispies treat when I spotted Thomas.

"Hey," he called, trudging across the field. "We need to make an extra stop at the paint store."

I was licking the remnants of my snack off my fingers when I heard the boys laughing on the other end of the field.

"Hey! Snow White! Here's your apple!"

I stood up just in time to see a blurry red object zing toward Thomas's head, whizzing past his hair.

Both Thomas and I screamed, equally high-pitched.

"Heads up! I mean, whoops!" Matt and his friends, in hysterics. They were wearing their *Outsiders* costumes. Which they weren't supposed to be wearing. Jeans that I had distressed for these idiots. White tanks I'd aged with tea bags and charcoal.

Which they were wearing because they were just doing what they always did.

Whatever they wanted.

Thomas looked down at the ground. "Oh," he said. "From yesterday. Right. Nice. I guess we—Monty? Montgomery!"

Thomas's voice was an echo. A distant vibration in the air that was already thickening around me. I started across the field toward them, my feet like big dinosaur feet, pounding the grass.

"Oh shit, buddy," some kid yukked. "You're in trouble now."

"Here she comes!"

They were prancing away. Not even away, just in wide circles. They moved in exaggerated strides, like a dance. Matt was at the center, walking, looking back, looking at me. He turned around. Put his hands up.

We were at a standoff. Five feet apart, our respective armies holding. Waiting.

"Chill out, Montgomery," he laughed. "I didn't hit him, okay? Don't get your tampon in a knot."

"Funny," I growled. *"You're so funny, Matt! You're so hilarious! What would this school do without you?"*

"Monty," Thomas called, his voice strained.

My heart was pounding so hard it felt like one of those punching bags boxers practice on, but trapped in the cage of my chest. *Punch, punch, punch.*

I closed my eyes. What did the card say?

> *In sight*
> *not see*
> *black light*
> *not be*

*"Hey,"* Matt called.

I opened my eyes.

"You know what's wrong with you? You dress like a dyke, and you can't take a joke."

"Why don't you just shut up?" I seethed.

"What?" Matt cupped his ear as he started to jog backward. "Sorry, I can't hear you."

"Tell her you don't speak lesbian," someone yelled.

"Tell her to shave her legs!"

I stepped forward. I reached up and grabbed the Eye, curled my fingers around it, tight. And I yelled, *"Shut your mouth! Don't even breathe! I swear to God if you make one more noise I will destroy you!"*

Matt stopped. Like, he froze. Like a cartoon character. One foot still hovering over the ground.

Then he fell to his knees. His fist pushed into his chest.

"Montgomery!" Suddenly, Thomas's hand was on my shoulder like an anvil.

Matt fell onto his side. My hand fell to my side.

His face was white against the green grass. His mouth opened wide. Like he was screaming. Like a fish out of water. Screaming with no sound coming out.

"Matt?" Thomas's voice caught. *"Matt!"*

Matt's friends came charging back. The grass squeaked under their shoes.

"Hey, Matt, man, you cool?"

"Matt?!"

"Oh my God."

They clustered around him, their voices swirling around in the wind, which had picked up and pushed against us, like a crowd. Like a riot.

*"Someone call an ambulance!"*

"What's going on?"

"Matt? What is it, man? *Matt!* Dude!"

"He can't talk, dude!"

Thomas pulled out his phone. "Nine-one-one? Yes. I think a student has had some sort of attack. Yes, we need an ambulance."

"Matt, just relax, man!"

"What's wrong with his face?"

Something, somewhere must have been burning. The air was full of a bonfire char smell. That smell of trees and nature turning into something else.

I stumbled away, across the field, across the baseball diamond. I dodged through the dwindling crowds of kids standing outside in the parking lot.

There were sirens. Kids stood by their cars, craning to see.

"What happened?"

"Did *you* see what happened?"

"Oh my *God*, an ambulance! What's going on?"

I walked up Main Street and through the suburban streets where parents still had their front doors wrapped in Day-Glo fake spiderwebs.

I wasn't sure where I was walking to, or why I hadn't waited for Thomas.

Or what had just happened.

I walked by Yoggy, but then I didn't want to go in there, either, so I just kept going.

Finally I headed to the movie plex and paid six dollars to see a James Bond movie. Because I suddenly had this idea that

I didn't want to be found, and there is no way someone would look for me in a James Bond movie.

I could feel my phone buzzing as James Bond ran across the screen and got beat up and put on a tux and took off his tux.

By the time I got out, I had two missed calls from my moms and a zillion texts from Thomas, one from Naoki.

Thomas: Where are you? Where did you go?
Thomas: Are you OK?
Thomas: Matt off to hospital.
Thomas: Where are you?
Thomas: Seriously.
Thomas: MONTY.
Thomas: Ignoring your best friend is lame.
Thomas: Okay. When you are ready you should call me.
Thomas: Call me now.
Thomas: Montgomery!!!! ☹
Thomas: Okay. Am peeved but will be patient for you to take your sweet time calling me back.
Thomas: Call me now.
Thomas: Montgomery, what happened?

Naoki's text was from three hours ago.

Naoki: you → ?

When I got home, Momma Jo was in the living room, watching TV.

"Where were you?" Momma Jo asked, standing up.

"We've been calling you." Mama Kate came in from the kitchen, holding up her phone. "Why didn't you answer?"

"Library."

Mama Kate dropped the phone by her side. Looked at Momma Jo.

"I can't answer the phone in the *library*," I snapped.

Everything looked a little different. A little off. Like the walls had been repainted a shade darker. Something.

"Hey." Momma Jo put her hands on her hips. "First of all, don't be a jerk to us. We are your *moms*. Second. If you see we have called, you can walk your butt out of the library and call us back."

I studied the carpet. "Fine. I'm going up to my room to study."

"More?" Momma Jo asked.

Mama Kate stepped forward. Then stopped.

"Yeah," I said.

"Monty," Mama Kate said. "We haven't seen you all day. Do you want to sit for a bit? Did you eat?"

"I ate. I have to study, okay?"

"Okay," Mama Kate said, stepping back toward the kitchen. "Okay, Monty. That's fine. Just . . ."

"Adjust your attitude a little would be nice," Momma Jo grumbled, settling into the La-Z-Boy.

*What is that supposed to mean?* I stewed.

As I passed Tesla's door, I could hear music blaring. Someone singing about love. And heartache.

In my room, I pulled everything I could find on the floor and the surrounding area onto my bed.

Curled up under the weight of a thousand cushions, I took the stone off my neck, wrapped my fingers around it. It was cold as ice. A little shiver ran through me.

What was happening?

# 9

☺ Hypnotism

HYPNOTISM IS THE ABILITY OF ONE PERSON TO SAY
"this is true," and make it true for another person.

Momma Jo doesn't believe in hypnotism, because she's only
ever seen white people get hypnotized. Which, basically, to
Momma Jo, means it's some sort of western society thing,
which somehow, to her, makes it less true. Which has something to do with feminism in this way I'm not completely sure
about.

I've tried it on Thomas many times, using instructions I
found on this website for the Society for the Secret Mind.
They didn't work. Thomas would always criticize my tone
and overall delivery, which he was convinced needed to be more
regal.

"Like Sherlock Holmes," he offered once, lying on my couch while Naoki filmed our session with her phone.

"I don't think it has anything to do with Sherlock Holmes," I countered. "You just want to hear a British accent."

"Your British accent is really funny," he said, eyes closed, waiting.

"Thomas."

"Just do it. I'll pretend to be hypnotized."

I tried it on Naoki after that, and she just fell asleep. But she said that in her dream, she was hypnotized.

"And it was really relaxing." She smiled.

☺ Difference between being asleep and being hypnotized? Can you be both?

Hypnotism is one of the few techniques I've seen videos of where it doesn't look completely fake. There are actual doctors out there who use hypnotism to help people remember stuff and also to help them quit smoking. Sometimes the people in these videos look dumb, but I think that's just because they're sort of sleeping, and sort-of-sleeping people look kind of dumb.

For anyone who says, you know, that magic isn't real, I say, okay, well, look at hypnotism. A hypnotist tells you, "You are getting sleepy," and you are. "You feel relaxed," and you are. A hypnotist counts to ten and says, "You are awake," and you are.

And no one is sure why.

It's a legit mystery.

Just because you don't understand something doesn't mean it's not happening.

Although that can be kind of scary.

When Naoki tried to hypnotize me, I fell asleep, or I thought I did. In the video, I just kept saying "Be careful" over and over again, in this sleepy voice, no matter what she asked me.

\* \* \*

The morning after what happened to Matt, I couldn't eat breakfast. I just got in the car and waited for Tesla to find her socks.

"You okay?" Momma Jo asked, twisting in her seat.

"Fine," I said, slumped down in the same overalls, this time in my I BELIEVE IN MAGIC T-shirt.

On my way to first period, I bumped into one of the boys from the soccer field. A friend of Matt's. Peter Hassle. A tall kid with long brown hair that was always in his eyes. Maroon spots on his face. Smelled like orange gum. Always the third kid to laugh at a joke about someone else.

He looked up and scooped the hair off his face. His eyes went from sleepy to wide awake in a nanosecond.

Like I'd just popped him in the face.

"Uh, sorry," he whispered, his gaze dropping to the floor.

By English, I could hear the whispers swirling on the backs of a thousand whispers.

"Didn't you know?"

"Montgomery Sole is obsessed with Matt Truit."

"Yesterday? She attacked him."

*"No!"*

"Josh and Pete told me."

"She's such a freak."

I pressed my fingers into my desk. The stone was still around my neck.

I'm sure I looked like a crazy person. I hadn't really slept. My joints felt like rotten apple cores; my head felt like a bowling ball balancing precariously in a divot between my shoulders. When I closed my eyes, I saw Matt, his face white as chalk, mouth stretched open. It felt like someone else's pulse was racing against mine, like the rumble of traffic outside.

Chairs squeaked against the floor as students settled. Someone had written *Matt Truit* on the chalkboard and circled his name with a big heart.

Naoki was nowhere to be seen that morning. I'd received two "are you ok?" texts from Thomas, who I'd also yet to see.

Me: I'm fine.

Thomas: Ok. I want to talk to you, OK?

Me: K.

It felt like time was slipping out from underneath me. Like I was in that hour of pre-sleep where you trip into a dream. In and out. Someone said something about a comic book.

*Right*, I thought, *because I'm in a classroom.*

"It's just a really good, uh, story," he finished. It was Teddy Kent. Who only ever talked about comic books. And super-heroes. In every class. No matter what we were talking about. "I thought. You know, better than the original series because well, the art is better in this one. At least. But the movie sucked."

Mrs. Farley leaned on her desk and flipped through her notebook.

"Okay. Great. Thanks, Teddy. Let's get back to the text, okay? I know you want to talk, but I'm not allowing any more comments on TV shows or comic books or music videos you like, unless you can link it to our discussion of the hero *in this book*. Okay. How do you know when a character is the hero of a story?"

Our crumpled copies of *The Outsiders* sat on our desks, spines cracked. Corners frayed. Some students made a show of flipping through their books, "looking" for the answers, as Mrs. Farley sat on her desk, tapping her pencil on her teeth the way she does when she's annoyed we're not raising our hands.

"The hero is the person who saves the day," someone shouted.

"It's the person who does good," one of the Parte sisters added.

"They have superpowers," someone in the back continued.

A Parte sister, possibly the same Parte sister, in the back of the room raised her hand. "Um, Mrs. Farley? Isn't a hero the person who overcomes *evil*?"

I felt there was a little bit of an excessive emphasis on *evil*. It ricocheted around the room and ended up bouncing on the floor and rolling under my desk.

"Maybe." Mrs. Farley paused. "Maybe. That's very interesting. Anyone else? Montgomery?"

"Maybe"—my mouth was a jar of cotton—"maybe the hero is the person who fights back."

More murmurs from the back.

"Interesting. Now, class. Hey. I said, '*Now*, class,' and that means eyes up *here*."

*Cue bell*, I thought. *Cue bell. Please.*

Then the bell rang.

* * *

Lunch felt like some psychedelic scene in some weird music video. I was supposed to go help Thomas, but instead I just bumped around the school like a zombie. Everyone felt too quiet or too loud. Like they were all acting. Or waiting. Or something. I could feel students' eyes on my back as I walked down the hall. I don't think I even meant to look in the door, but then I heard a familiar voice.

And there was Naoki standing in the physics lab, talking to Kenneth White. She was wearing a white smock, a white stocking hat, and what looked like white cowboy boots. Hugging a book to her chest and holding another book out to him. And she was smiling.

I must have made a noise because Kenneth turned his head to look out the door.

I stepped back, a giant step, bumping into someone who shoved me forward.

*"Hey!"*

Inside the classroom, I heard Naoki say, "Who was that?" Something about her tone. Like I must have been an intruder.

I guess I kind of ran down the hallway.

What was she saying to Kenneth? Maybe something about me?

Somehow I made it to class for my second bio test of the month. The heart. Which I had studied, though not recently. I remembered most of it. It's amazing that tests are basically just these flimsy pieces of paper. On which you're supposed to put these names of things that you're supposed to have memorized.

Ventricles. Aortas.

I colored in the veins with a black marker. Then I colored the whole thing in, with a series of spiraling strokes.

I looked over and noticed Naoki looking at me from her desk. I felt the corners of my mouth turn down. Naoki's eyes widened.

*Hey*, she mouthed.

I looked back down. Curled over my drawing.

After we handed in our papers, a little paper square landed on my desk.

*me → ? ← you*

I crumpled it up and walked out.

Whatever Naoki was doing with Kenneth, I didn't care. Let him be her new friend. They both liked white. They would be perfect together. They could honeymoon somewhere even whiter. In a cloud. A perfect cloud of "why should I care?"

Study hall was like some sort of torture test, pretending to read while I basically just watched the clock tick. Finally, I got a pass and went to the bathroom to splash some cold water on my face and do what you would normally do in a bathroom—escape—when Madison walked in.

She was talking to the Parte twins, but as soon as they spotted me, they all stopped talking. One of the Partes went to go to the sink, but Madison put her arm across the front of her, like a human seat belt, and whispered loudly, "Wait till she's gone."

I turned. "Can I help you, Madison?"

Madison's voice was quiet but sure. "I told my mom what happened to Matt. What you did. My mom said you'll never understand the difference between right and wrong, because you come from a broken family," she said. "So. I should feel sorry for you."

I had to close my eyes. The world was trembling.

"My family is not broken!" I screamed.

There was a gasp. Something dropped to the ground and shattered. A soda bottle or something. Foam spread across the floor. I looked up. It felt like the room was about to boil. I could feel my eyes darting from Parte twin to Parte twin to Madison. I looked down and the tiles rippled and swam in front of my eyes.

I tripped forward and slammed through the bathroom door.

By the time I got to the front doors of the school, I was running.

* * *

When I got to Yoggy, Tiffany was behind the counter, wearing a weird-looking, frumpy sweatshirt. It was too big, and she had the sleeves rolled up. She looked tired. Her dreads were all limp and hanging around her face like . . . limp dreads, basically.

"Hey," I said.

"Did you run here? You look like crap." Tiffany sighed, pushed a cup in my direction. "Go ahead. Take all you want. My treat. I'm quitting."

"What?" I grabbed a cup and started in with some Banana Sensation swirled with Orange You Glad.

"Yeah, I'm leaving in a week." Tiffany rubbed her eyes. "I'm going home."

*What?* The spiral of pink and yellow continued to pour into my cup, folding over and over itself until I realized I was letting it overflow. "Crap."

"Uh, yeah. Take it easy. You can have two cups. Take as much as you want."

Holding the cup steady with two hands, I walked carefully to the nearest table. "This isn't your home?"

Tiffany shook her dreads. "My mom's in Michigan. I'm gonna go live in her basement till I can get my . . . you know, my situation straightened out."

"What situation?"

"You know," Tiffany said as she snatched a handful of mini marshmallows from the tray. "Anxiety and stuff. Since I left school. All of that. I'm not sleeping. All I eat is this crap."

Looking down at her hand, she walked over and flicked the marshmallows into the garbage can.

"See what I mean?" she said. "I need to eat a salad."

My face must have frozen. "A salad? This is California."

"Look, Monty. It's not that simple, okay? You just thought I was some genius who happened to be working a minimum-wage job in a hamlet in California after leaving a master's degree?" She shifted a few chairs back into place around the tables before sinking into the chair across from mine. "You thought that was just my idea of a good time?"

The tips of my fro-yo were melting, losing their crisp swirly edge and oozing little orange-and-banana tears.

"I just thought you were working on your, you know, your research on the, you know, the SorBetties . . ." The smell of melting yogurt wafted up from my bowl. Like gum. Old gum.

"Right. My research. Yeah, well. It's not healthy." Tiffany looked at my bowl and raised an eyebrow.

"No toppings," she said. "Interesting."

"Yeah, I'm good." My voice echoed from somewhere under my angry stomach.

"You know, last night, I was up all night. Thinking, like, you know, no one cares about"—Tiffany sighed—"oppression. It makes me so mad. All these women, all they care about is being skinny. That's it. They don't care about anything else. They watch their calories because if they weren't doing that, they'd actually have to do something. They'd have to think about themselves and all these things they take for granted about the world around them. And they don't want to."

"Yeah," I grumbled, still not eating but adamantly stirring my frozen yogurt into liquid. "It's like, get a life."

Tiffany placed her palms flat on the table. "Yeah, and I'm just as bad because I hate them all."

Under the flickering fluorescent lights, Tiffany's face was looking a little yellow. Not unlike the color of the soupy mess of banana and orange I had created but would not be eating. Possibly feeling my gaze, she looked up. Squinted. The machines whirred as we stared across the room at each other.

Her eyes like onyx.

"Well." I was determined not to blink. "Maybe some people deserve to be hated."

Tiffany stood up, shoving her chair back. Shooting me a look, a mean look, like I'd said the worst, dumbest thing. Like I'd just said that foreshadowing can only happen after dinner.

I sat back, pushing my cup away. *What even made me think Tiffany was so cool, anyway?* I thought. Just because she hated skinny yoga chicks didn't mean she got what it was like to live here. Like, live here being a kid who has no choice but to deal with these people every day.

Tiffany dropped her hands by her sides. "Do you even hear what I'm saying, Monty?"

It was all too much. I just started backing out of there. "Well, it sucks you're leaving," I said. "Thanks for the yogurt."

"Yeah." Tiffany turned and headed into the back room. "Later."

As soon as I got outside, I realized I'd just left my cup there. Like some stupid SorBetty.

But I couldn't go back in.

I started walking. Past the bus stop. I tried to focus on my footsteps, to match them with my heartbeat, which is something I read is helpful for . . . something. Maybe mind-body control.

At some point I looked up.

There he was. Taped to an old newspaper box. The Reverend White.

"Oh, of course," I said, leaning in to stare the reverend down. "Of course you're right here! *Of course! Hello! Nice to see you again and again!*"

## THE REVEREND WHITE IS HERE TO HELP YOU TAKE THE PATH TO SALVATION

I didn't even want to touch it with my hands. I stepped back and pulled it down with the toe of my boot, leaving half of it dangling.

When I got home this time, Momma Jo and Mama Kate were waiting. The principal called, Mama Kate said. Because I'd left early. Skipped study hall. Was reportedly having trouble in both Bio and English. Plus he said he'd heard some students talking about how whatever had happened to Matt Truit had started with an altercation. With me.

I dropped my bag. "They said I hit him?"

Momma Jo looked at Mama Kate. "No, he said 'altercation,' not that that makes any sense to me. He said some students saw you fighting with Matt before he collapsed. Is that true?"

"No. I mean, I was there. But I didn't. I didn't hit him."

I tried to take in their faces, which were a mix of twisted and concerned. Did they think I hit him?

The living room clock *ticktock*ed.

"Okay." Momma Jo looked up at Mama Kate. "We didn't think you hit him. It just seems like . . . Maybe something else happened. Which you can, of course, tell us. And you *should* tell us." It sounded for a second like Momma Jo was trying to convince Mama Kate. "He's in the hospital, Monty."

"Because of me?" My throat felt like it was closing, cutting off air to my brain. I tried to stare at a spot right behind my moms so I could look up, without having to actually look at them.

"No," Mama Kate said, hesitantly I thought. "Just . . . Monty, he's still very ill."

"We just don't get along," I said quietly. "But I didn't. I didn't do anything to him."

They looked at each other. Sending lesbian mom psychic signals.

"The principal also said there was some damage to your locker," Momma Jo said.

I looked down at my boots. I could feel Mama Kate staring at the top of my head.

"Why are you skipping class?" Mama Kate said softly. "Monty, it just seems like there's something happening here. All this . . ."

"It's just study hall." I shrugged. "Everyone skips." I started sending out my own psychic signal.

*Please just send me to my room.*

"Um, and the locker," I added. "Yeah. No. It's just old paint. It's always been there. It's a crappy school."

*Please just send me to my room.*

I'm sure there's no kid who wants to talk to their mom or moms or dads or whatever about the crappy stuff that goes on with them and crappy people at school. I'm sure that's just true. I know Thomas never tells his parents anything, because he says he doesn't like talking about the inevitable.

Upstairs, I could hear Tesla jogging on the spot to pop music.

"Do I have to go to the principal's office?"

Momma Jo and Mama Kate exchanged looks again. "No," Momma Jo said. "We just wanted to check in with you."

"Monty," Mama Kate whispered. "Is it the posters? The Reverend White?"

I shoved my hands into my pockets. *Just look at them*, I thought. *Look calm.* If you can look at them and look calm, they'll think everything is fine, and then this will all be over.

I took a deep breath. Looked up. Looked at Mama Kate. Looked at Momma Jo. "No," I said. "It's nothing. Everything's fine. I'm just tired. I'd really just like to go to bed."

"Okay. Can I give you a kiss?" Mama Kate pulled on the ties on her sweatshirt.

"Yeah."

Mama Kate tentatively walked over and gave me a hug and a kiss on the head. Which made me feel . . .

Kind of terrible.

Maybe that's terrible to say.

But how much more terrible would it be if I told them everything?

Pretty terrible.

I went upstairs.

And there, on Tesla's door . . . was a cross.

A cross.

I pounded on her door until it swung open.

"What is *this*?" I snapped, jabbing my finger at the cross. It looked like the same cross I'd pried off my locker a week ago.

"Mama Kate said it's okay," Tesla said, her face sweaty from her jog, her eyes fixed and fierce.

"Why do you want a cross?" I hissed, jabbing my finger at the door.

Tesla put her hands on her hips. A single curl stuck to her forehead. "Because I do. Because I want to pray. It's not a big deal. Mama Kate said it was okay."

"Where did you get it? Did you get it from the Reverend White?" My lips were going numb.

"Hey, what's going on up there?" Momma Jo called from downstairs. "Monty?"

"I don't even know who that is. I got it from Mary at school!" Tesla screamed.

*"Mary who?"*

"Stop yelling at me!"

And she slammed the door closed. It shut about a hair away from my face. Leaving me face-to-face with a melted-looking Jesus.

*"You don't need to slam the door!"* I fumed, and I turned and ran to my room.

"What is going on?" The house shook as Momma Jo pounded up the stairs.

*"Nothing!"* I screamed from my room, slamming the door.

Two seconds later, there was more pounding, this time on my door. "Monty!" Momma Jo hollered.

My fortress felt small that day. Like a tiny wall of cushions that would never protect me from how messed up the world was. "Just leave me alone, okay? Please?"

I could hear Momma Jo sigh. Then a murmuring behind her.

"Okay. Monty. We love you," Mama Kate said. Her voice sounded heavy and sad.

I pulled a pillow over my head and tried to make myself disappear.

"You are getting sleepy," I whispered. "You are getting tired."

It didn't work. It doesn't always.

I pulled the stone off my neck and pressed it against my cheek. It was still cold.

\* \* \*

Me: Thomas?

Thomas: Yes?

Me: You're still my friend, right? You're not going to change and become some Christian freak and start hating me or something are you?

Thomas: What are you talking about?

Me: R u my friend?

Thomas: I'm your friend. Where were you today? I looked for you and someone said you took off. Find me tomorrow okay?

Me: Ok.

And after all that, I put the stone back around my neck and went to bed.

# 10

"UNFORTUNATELY, IT APPEARS MR. TRUIT WILL NO longer be able to take part in our theatrical production," Mr. Gyle stammered, then coughed. Then looked around the room. "Due to illness."

Eyes wandered in my direction.

Matt Truit was still not back in school. I wondered if he was any better. Clearly, it was bad enough that the principal called my parents. Even though it was also clear no one knew what had happened.

Including me, really.

The card said something about black light and "not be." But wouldn't "not be" mean dead?

"Eyes front, class!"

Could I have killed him?

Matt Truit had an understudy, but it turned out the

understudy was just doing it to hang out with Matt and thought the idea of actually being onstage acting was, in his words, "gay."

Sipping from his massive water bottle, Mr. Gyle tried a weak smile. "Ah, so, kids." He looked like *he'd* had a heart attack.

I wondered if Mrs. Farley was getting sick of his pre-class announcements.

"I'm actually, uh, on my knees here, folks." He chuckled nervously.

"I'm sure someone will be up for the job," Mrs. Farley said, stepping forward and opening the door for him to leave.

Which he seemed to do kind of grudgingly.

*Maybe they had a thing,* I thought.

Mrs. Farley turned back to the class. "Okay. Now, let's see if we can get through this novel. Who wants to start with the homework questions?"

On my way out of English, I spotted Naoki gliding toward me across the hall. Her hair was tied up in a bunch of white ribbons that flapped behind her.

"You're not talking to me," she said, slowing down next to me.

"Looks like I'm talking to you now," I said, speeding up slightly.

"I want to ask if everything is okay. But I *know okay* is a bad word. Because it doesn't really mean anything. *O* and *K*." Naoki paused, jogging a little to keep up with me.

We turned the corner and ran into a crowd of students.

"Don't really have anything to say," I called over the noise.

Naoki touched my arm. "Hey," she said. "Stop please?"

The wave of students trampled past.

"I have chemistry," I said, looking down the hall.

Someone was skateboarding. I could hear the wheels grinding on the floor. "Okay. Well, I wanted to say that I didn't ask Kenneth to be in the Mystery Club," Naoki said, looking into my eyes. "I want to make sure you and Thomas are both comfortable with it."

Another two-hundred-pound pause. The sound of wheels faded.

Naoki shifted. The crystal she was wearing around her neck spilled little rainbows onto her face. It made me think of the time Thomas decided we should have an *Alien* party and Naoki showed up with binoculars because she thought we were literally going to see aliens. When Thomas pulled out the *Alien* DVDs, it was the first time I saw her be kind of bummed out.

Finally, I asked, because I was actually curious, "Why do you like him?"

Naoki frowned. "Kenneth. Yes. He's smart. He likes to read interesting things. He's like a map to a place I didn't know existed. Just like you."

Naoki was thinking maps. All I could think of was posters. "He doesn't want to save us all?"

Naoki looked up at the ceiling. "Saved. Hmmm. Saved. Saved."

I know she was just feeling the word over, but hearing it repeated like that, like some sort of chant, was freaking me out.

Finally she looked at me. "I just feel like we're all supposed to connect. I really just feel it."

The halls were empty. Which always feels like a kind of no-man's-land to me. An unnatural territory.

I turned. Shifted my bag on my shoulder. "Okay. Well. Like I said, I gotta go."

* * *

Despite not having a lead, Jefferson High's production of *The Outsiders* did have a fantastic set, which I worked on that day while auditions went on during lunch.

Thomas seemed relieved to have me in the backstage area, his domain, where he could just give me little tasks to do and, I was pretty sure, keep an eye on me. Mostly I half watched the auditions and half painted. It looked like the new lead role was between Kevin Barton, the goalie from the soccer team, who looked the part but also looked like he didn't want to be there, and Percy Moffatt, whose name pretty much says it all. Percy spent most of his time playing piano, and Thomas said he was only auditioning because he found out he needed some school activities on his application to Harvard.

"And he doesn't want to paint sets?" I asked, smoothing out the tarp underneath what felt like the billionth wall I'd painted for this thing.

"I don't think you can paint sets in cashmere pants." Thomas snorted. Which was a little odd because why would Thomas of all people disdain a cashmere pant?

Thomas was painting a drive-in sign. Which was going to be strung with little lights so it would look like a real sign.

"Hey," I said, dabbing my brush in gray. "Is Percy gay?"

"Uh, no." Thomas finished the curve of the *D*. "It seems that Percy is one of the few Percys alive who is not gay."

"Are you sure?"

"Very sure." Thomas left his sign and walked over, peering at my wall. "Is that the same gray as from the last group?"

"Yes. How can you be very sure? About Percy?"

Thomas stood back and squinted at the wall. "Because we went for coffee, and I thought he was flirting with me, so I kissed him goodbye, and he shoved me and called me a fag. I think his parents are superreligious or something."

He turned his head slightly, walked away, walked back toward the wall. Sighed. "It looks like a different gray."

I tried to catch Thomas's eye, but he was lost in gray. "That sucks," I said.

"Well, you wanted to know why I only date older men, there you have it. Stop painting. I want to make sure it's the right color."

It was around three thirty when I finally left the theater, in search of Thomas, who'd left to find some "better" gray paint. It was last-bell time. Cheerleaders grabbed pom-poms; jocks grabbed gear. Band geeks grabbed appropriately shaped black suitcases. Lockers slammed.

I walked and texted my way through the corridors, bumping past kids headed for various games and home.

Me: Where did u go? It's just gray paint. Can I go home and we'll do it tomorrow?

Me: If you don't answer, I'm leaving.

Me: 5, 4, 3, 2 . . .


I turned the corner.

There, just down the hall, stood Kenneth White and the Reverend White. The reverend was at least six feet tall. Taller than Kenneth. A tower. He was wearing a pale blue suit, matching his white hair.

He was right there. In the flesh.

At some point, the crowd pulled away from me and I was alone in the hall. That was when Kenneth looked up. His face was like a statue's. Stone. Cold. Kenneth looked up, and he pointed.

At me.

The Reverend White looked up. His eyes narrowed.

In a flash I remembered the one and only time I spent a day with Mama Kate's parents alone. I think I was, like, four. This was pre-Tesla. Back when we still lived in Canada. I remember they didn't stay in the house, because Mama Kate said they wanted to stay at the Holiday Inn. The first day of their visit, they took me on a special "grandparents-only" visit to a kiddie park.

Most of the day was okay. I had my first cotton candy, and my grandfather even let me get a Coke because he said it was a special day.

It all fell apart when my grandfather decided I should go on a pony ride. Like, ten seconds after the ride started, I freaked out because my pony kept trotting and it felt like the earth was shaking. And I started to cry, and they had to stop and pull me off.

"I want BOBO!" I screamed. "I want Bobo NOW!"

"Stop screaming!" My grandfather took my arms and tried to force them to my sides. His hands were hard and scratchy like a rug. His face went from soft and pink to red. Up close I noticed his nose had a weird freckle on it that was raised. He had eyebrows with long, curly white hairs that seemed to reach toward me when his face got close to mine.

I'd never had a man grab me like that. Or yell. I started to scream and twist, and everyone turned and looked at us. I tried to kick him so I could get free, and he closed his grip tighter.

"BOBO!" I wailed.

"She means Jo," my grandmother whispered, clutching her purse to her chest.

"That woman," my grandfather said, his voice low like some sort of engine, "is not your mother."

"It's okay," my grandmother whispered. "Don't cry. Please don't cry."

I remember dust on the toes of my new red shoes as we walked to the parking lot, my grandfather holding my hand tight.

"Would you want to come live with us someday?" my grandmother asked, handing me a piece of cotton candy that promptly melted against my skin and turned me blue.

I remember they had a big yellow car with windows you had to roll down with a handle. But I wasn't allowed to roll mine down.

"No escaping!" my grandmother sang. And then she gave me a Kleenex because my nose was running all over the place.

"Child has no father," my grandfather grumbled. I watched his head shake from my view in the backseat. The back of his neck looked like a bunch of skinny plain doughnuts all stacked up on top of each other.

I sniffled.

"A child needs a father." He shook his head.

When we got to my house, my grandfather wouldn't come inside. He helped me out of the car and kissed my head. Then he stood by the curb as my grandmother walked me to the house. I remember turning back and seeing him squinting at me. Not waving.

Back in the hallway, the Reverend White frowned.

Of course, I always knew the Reverend White was real. But it was different, knowing he was real and seeing his posters everywhere, and having him in my school. At my school. Staring at him squinting at me, I felt like I was losing oxygen, losing ground.

Following Kenneth's finger, he stood straight and started walking toward me.

I turned and ran down the hall, darted into the gym, around the back, through the eighth-grade hallway, and into the back lot. I could feel the stone clanging against my chest.

I ran until I couldn't feel my footfalls, just a thundering

pounding beneath my waist. In the distance, I heard a tweet from the football practice on the far field. I took off around the school, scanning the horizon for the Reverend White. I could feel him striding toward me, legs stiff, arms out, like some sort of Christian Frankenstein.

I circled back toward the south parking lot—and ran right into Kenneth White.

It was like a particle collision, a burst of energy that sent us both flying back and onto our butts. I scrambled to my feet as fast as I could.

Kenneth pulled himself to his feet, dusted off his hands. "Watch yourself," he said.

"Watch *myself*?" I gasped. "Are you serious?"

Kenneth shook his head. Walked over to his bag and picked it up.

The gravel slid under my feet as I paced.

*In sight*
*not see*
*black light*
*not be*

Kenneth looked up.

"Excuse me, *preacher*," I spat. My heart was beating so fast I could hear it in my lips.

"Don't . . ." Kenneth said, his voice low.

"Don't *what*?" I cut in, stepping forward, reaching to wrap my fingers around the Eye. "You got something to say?"

Kenneth shook his head, dusted off his bag. Coolly. "Nope," he said.

"Montgomery!" Thomas and Naoki, in chorus, came running around the corner.

"What's going on?" Naoki gasped.

"Yeah. Tell them." I pointed at Kenneth. "Tell them why you were pointing at me. Tell them why you were pointing me out *to your dad*!"

Kenneth looked at Naoki and back at me. He was still holding his bag over his shoulder.

"I was walking," I said, turning to Thomas, "down the hall and this homophobe *pointed me out* to his *father*."

Thomas kept his eyes steady on me like he was trying to read my insides.

"Tell me that's not true," I said, pointing at Kenneth. "God's honest truth. That's a thing, right?"

"*Augh!*" Naoki threw her bag down. It made a terrible, crashing, glass-breaking noise.

"Oh," Thomas said.

Naoki knelt down and opened her bag. Inside were thick-cut, broken pieces of glass. "It was a crystal ball," she said, to the broken pieces mostly.

Kenneth stepped toward her. "You okay?"

"How about you just get out of here?" I barked. "No one wants you here. Why don't you just go back to church and get homeschooled or whatever it is you do?"

Naoki stood over her bag. "What is wrong with you?" she whispered.

She was talking . . . to me.

Naoki's eyes searched my face. Her cheeks were all flushed and pink. Her voice rose. "Why are you acting like this?"

My eyes were practically popping out of my head. *Now* she was taking *his* side? Actually standing there, in front of him, and calling me out?

"You know what?" I sneered. "When it's your family that people are attacking, then maybe you'll get it."

"You don't know what you're talking about," Naoki said. "You think you're the only person who's ever been oppressed or hurt or treated badly because of who you are?" Naoki pressed her hands to her face.

"Naoki," Thomas whispered, reaching over to touch her shoulder.

"*No!*" Naoki pulled away, glaring at me. "*You!*" Naoki's voice hit a shout. Then got quiet. "*You* should know better."

Then, I swear to God, she walked over to Kenneth and said, in a regular, non-mad voice, "Let's go."

"You know what?" I screeched, "You suck! I should know better? The only thing I clearly don't know is how to pick a *friend.*"

I turned and started speed-walking away from the school, away from Naoki and everyone else at Jefferson, as fast as I could.

I didn't hear Thomas running behind me until he was right by my shoulder.

"Okay. Let's go," he said. He grabbed my arm, steering me across the street.

I tried to tug my arm out of his grip. "What are you doing? *Hey!*"

Thomas stopped. "I'm taking you for a talking-to, Montgomery Sole," he said. "Now, let's go." He picked up my arm again, this time gently, and turned us toward the park. "This is the part of the movie where we get serious."

* * *

We went to Thomas's favorite park. Breakup park. The park where I took him for all his breakups. A tiny park of no more than twelve square feet of grass and a few trees. A bench of warped wood and iron.

Thomas dumped me onto the bench, then sat down next to me, folding his arms. "Okay. Now, tell me what's happening."

I stared at the cuffs of my pants, which were covered in dust. "Well, Naoki just yelled at me."

"Montgomery." Thomas adjusted himself so he was sitting cross-legged, facing me.

"What?" I spun around.

A gust of wind must have filled Thomas's lungs and exploded out of him. *"Jesus, Montgomery, what is going on with you?"* Thomas sat back. "Okay. I'm sorry. I shouldn't yell. Just, tell me what is going on?"

"Well," I fumed, "let's see. We've got someone who thinks we're all going to hell postering the city with, like, 'Save the American Family' crap. Which you don't think is a big deal."

"What does that have to do with Kenneth?" Thomas asked.

I jumped up off the bench. There was so much electricity

stabbing at my insides I couldn't keep still. "Kenneth White is the *son* of Reverend White. Does it seem all that far-fetched to you that the son of the hater of gays would eventually have *something* to say about the queers at Jefferson High?"

"The Reverend White . . ." Thomas started.

"No one at this school will care about us getting screwed but us, Thomas!" I started to pace. "Crosses up on the lockers, no one cares. Matt Truit calls you a fag, no one cares. *No one* cares, *no one* at Jefferson High is going to do anything about it."

A bunch of little kids were playing in the park on the swings. The sky was turning gray. A little ribbon of cold wrapped around my neck. I plonked myself back down on the bench and tried to pull my legs in to get warm.

Thomas sat, quiet. Then he said, "Did you do something to him? To Matt? That day?"

"I didn't touch him." Thomas's eyes were boring little holes in my soul. I looked down. "I mean, it's possible that the Eye might have done something, but . . ."

"What are you talking about?"

"The Eye . . ." *The Eye what?* I thought.

Thomas's eyes narrowed. "The Eye? What happened to sharing your insights with the Mystery Club? I thought we were exploring the bounds of reality together. I thought we were all going to *wield.*"

"We're painting sets this week," I said.

"Okay, well, now I'm all ears. Tell me about your Eye."

"I don't know what it is. Sometimes, when I'm mad. And I hold it. Stuff happens."

"What stuff?" Thomas leaned forward. "Monty."

"It only happens when I'm wearing the Eye." My hands flailed, then dropped, useless, into my lap. "I don't know exactly what *it* is."

I told Thomas about the last few days. The images in my head were scattered on the floor like some sort of terrible collage. What happened first? What happened after the box arrived? Then High Bun disappearing off the bleachers? And Matt? How did I even know what was happening?

Thomas furrowed his brow. "So *it* happened more than once."

I bowed my head, which was suddenly like a brick. "I guess."

*Naoki would understand*, I thought.

Then another thought hit me like a movie punch to the stomach. *No, she wouldn't.* She was probably hanging out with Kenneth right now. Talking about me.

Thomas appeared to be deep in serious thought. He stared at me like I was an exam. I got the feeling that he was ready to chase me down if I made a break for it. "Where is it now? The stone. The Eye of Know."

"Safe," I said.

Thomas nodded. "Okay. Okay. So get rid of it."

"What?"

"Montgomery."

I shook my head.

"Montgomery, if you do, in fact, have a stone that is causing harm to people. In *any* way. Why would you hold on to it?"

Two girls with ice cream cones stopped in midwalk and midlick to stare at Thomas and me.

So we stopped for a sec.

Till they kept licking and walking.

I stared. At Thomas. "I'm not getting rid of it."

It didn't even occur to me it was true until I said it. Because even if I didn't understand what the Eye was doing, I felt like it was going to keep me safe. Because even if I didn't understand why, it felt powerful. Protecting.

And I was not safe. Maybe no one I loved was safe. Not with all this stuff going on. Not with "Save the American Family," not with Kenneth. Maybe I was never safe. Not ever.

I needed it.

"Okay," Thomas snapped. "Here's the thing. I don't know what this stone is or does or this Eye or whatever. But it is clear to me that you *think* it might be doing bad things to people. And it is freaking me out that that is *not* freaking you out. And let's just say that this—*this*—is exactly how being a villain starts. Villains are people who are pissed off and who get enough power to do something about it. And then they *do that thing* even though that thing is *hurting someone*."

My cheeks burned. "I'm the *villain*. Seriously? You can go to this school and deal with this crap and think that *I'm* the villain? That's messed up."

There was a long silence, during which the temperature dropped at least one more degree.

"I know it's bad sometimes, Monty." Thomas reached forward. I scooted back. "But it doesn't make things any better to . . . hate them, like this. It's just . . . it's a black hole, Monty. It's not worth it."

"Well. I hate them anyway," I said.

Thomas looked up to the sky. "You know, I vowed long ago never to let some stupid kids make me bitter at a young age. That's why they don't touch me. Because I won't let them. You shouldn't, either."

Thomas scanned the park, presumably taking in the little kids playing. The moms and strollers. The citizens of Aunty. "Do you remember when we first met?"

"Of course." It was right after the Jefferson Middle School and High School merged. I was in seventh grade, and he was in eighth grade, but I saw him in the halls, walking to class, all the time. He had this crazy jacket on that was black and white checkers. Long, skinny black pants that were so tight I thought they were leggings. Lots of other kids thought they were leggings, too. Sometimes he wore a top hat. Sometimes that top hat had a feather in it.

It was his circus phase.

"You know, of course, that I did not want to be here. And that saying 'I did not want to be here' is a gross understatement." Thomas shook his head. "When we moved to Aunty I remember pummeling the front steps of the house we moved into like, 'This is *not* San Francisco!'" For dramatic effect, Thomas shook his fists at the sky.

"Tragedy," I mumbled.

"Don't mock. This is a serious story, Montgomery. Listen to my tone. Very serious. So. I thought I was doomed. Kicked out of the synchro team Olympic pool and dumped into a kiddie pool of Target shoppers."

"That's being kind."

"I thought the possibility of finding signs of intelligent life here were slim to none," Thomas continued. "But then there you were. My miracle."

"Yeah."

"So I was not expecting you, and there you were."

I squinted, turning Thomas into a blur. "So what are you saying?"

Thomas shrugged. "I'm saying, I don't know, you can't know everything and everyone, Monty."

My insides were bubbling.

"Oh yeah? How about this? The first time we met, you were sitting on the steps, crying. Because some idiot drew a picture of you in the bathroom. Remember that?"

It was drawn in thick black marker. Thomas in his tight leggings and his big pompadour hair. And they had written, *Thomas blow jobs for $5!*

Thomas took a deep breath. Blew it out slowly.

"Tell me things have changed. Tell me I'm wrong about the good students of Jefferson High."

"Okay," Thomas said, his voice teetering on exasperated. "Okay. Well, how about this? I'm not saying he's the greatest guy in the world, but it seems to me like you're pissed off at Kenneth White for no reason. As far as I can see, all Kenneth is trying to do is pass math. I don't think he's the one who glued the cross to your locker, and I think you need to chill out on Naoki, who just wants to be his friend because she knows what it's like to be the new guy."

I pulled my knees up to my chin. "Naoki just wants a boyfriend."

"I don't think it's like that," Thomas said. "Naoki is your friend, Monty. So am I."

I stood up.

I could feel the tears streaming down my cheeks and catching the cold of the wind. "My sister, Thomas, *my sister* is praying with one of those White crosses now! This whole world is just too messed up. I'm not a villain, Thomas. I'm just the only person who can see . . ."

"What?" Thomas asked.

*What's coming.*

My phone rang. Moms' call.

I reached down and flipped my phone to silent.

"Montgomery." Thomas grabbed my hand. His face was all swimming with some sort of sad that was hurting my insides to see. "Don't leave. Let's go for a walk or something."

"This sucks," I said.

It did.

And it was getting late.

And my heart hurt.

So I left.

# 11

A COLD WIND STALKED ME DOWN THE STREET, PUSHING
my hair into my face and making me wish I had something
other than long sleeves on.

I walked the long way home so I could go through my favorite street. I like it because it has big trees and, when kids are
at school, it's quiet. Like superquiet.

The trees are huge, so you can feel kind of small and pro-
tected.

And, like I said, it's quiet.

Momma Jo said that when they first moved to California,
she was a little freaked out. Then she discovered how quiet it
can be here, because there's enough space around for people
to go to their own separate areas to be whoever they want to
be and make whatever noise they want.

"So I can go be pissed off somewhere nice and quiet," she'd say.

"Then come back and have dinner," Mama Kate would always add.

At some point I realized I was heading home, and I stopped.

Had Kenneth White reported me to the principal? Probably.

Picturing my moms talking to the principal about me, *again*, and feeling all worried and disappointed felt like a punch. I couldn't take one more person looking at me like Thomas. Like Naoki.

I couldn't go home. What would I say? Mama Kate would be a wreck. Plus who knew what else was going on with Tesla and her cross now?

I turned around and started walking I-don't-know-where. My brain was mush. Like old oatmeal that someone leaves in the sink, and then it gets water in it and it looks disgusting.

Life sucks when you don't know where you're going, by the way. When you're just walking and you don't know when you're going to be able to stop. Because you don't have anywhere to go.

If I were a crier, it would have made me cry.

Instead it just made me feel cold.

I wished I had a cushion fort I could just crawl into, be muffled into silence.

Muffled into nothing.

I walked for about an hour, pretty much across town. Past

little shops, and the hardware store, and the new yoga place, and the old yoga place. I walked till my feet burned and I had to crash on a bench by Pete's Taco, which was closed because someone found a really big fingernail in their taco last week. At least that was what I heard.

Next to Pete's Taco was an office where the AA people used to meet before they got moved to the mall. There was a light on behind the blinds. That was when I saw the sign taped to the door.

## VIGIL FOR THE AMERICAN FAMILY
## SAVE YOUR COUNTRY
## SAVE YOUR SOUL
## HERE!
## TONIGHT @ 7 PM

I pulled out my phone. 7:35 p.m. Five missed calls. Texts from Thomas and my moms.

The door was shut, but I could see a light on through the blinds. Before I could take a step forward, the door swung open and Percy came out. He was wearing bright blue pants and a blue-and-red-striped sweater. Like a French flag. Cashmere, probably. He put his head down and shoved his hands in his pockets. Then he turned right and disappeared down the street.

Percy. The non-gay who looks like a gay. What was he doing there? I thought of texting Thomas. But then I'd have to talk to him. And explain where I was.

And that would probably not be good.

I waited. I could feel myself breathing, harder than a charging horse.

The sound of Percy's fancy shoes *clip-chip*ping against the sidewalk faded.

This was it. This was, like, the vortex of the Reverend White. Where he was gathering his troops to defend the American family. Against my family. He was probably in there, talking about sin and how gays aren't human and they're perverts.

Right now.

I looked at the building, hard. I wanted the whole thing to disappear. To explode. At that moment, I wanted to destroy it and everyone in it. *Screw them all*, I thought. What made anyone think anything like that was okay, attacking people they didn't even know? Because of some ridiculous religious belief.

*In sight*
*not see*
*black light*
*not be*

*Not be, not be, not be.*

Nothing.

Maybe it only worked on people.

Except it didn't work on Kenneth.

*What if it worked on everyone but the Whites?* I thought.

Great. The one group of people it would be good to obliterate.

*That's what you want to do?* Thomas's voice was a whisper in my skull. *Destroy a building of people? Villain much?*

I felt my feet move before I decided where I was going. Step by step, I got closer to the door and finally closed my fingers around the metal handle.

*Maybe.*

*Yes.*

Inside it was so quiet you could hear a pin drop.

There were rows and rows of chairs set up, plastic chairs like the ones teachers put out on parents' night. Someone had set them up for at least forty. Each chair had a flyer on it.

## Prayer for the American Family.
## God bless me with the wisdom to know
## your will. And the strength to see your
## will be done.

"Welcome."

He was wearing his signature white suit. Up close, his hair was gray and thinning. He had icy blue eyes and a perfect white-toothed smile. He looked like someone advertising the perfect household cleaner.

He took my hand and shook it with a strong squeeze. He smelled like baby powder.

"Uh, hello?" I said.

*Do you know me?* I thought.

"I'm very glad to see you here today," the Reverend contin-ued, squeezing harder. "You know who else is glad?"

"Jesus?" I guessed.

"Yes! I believe so," the Reverend chuckled. "Are you here to pray with us today?"

His voice was warm. Like soup.

"No," I said. "I mean no, I—"

"You just happened to be in the neighborhood." He chuckled again. This time it was kind of a Santa Claus chuckle, except kind of forced. Like a mall Santa Claus. A mall Santa Claus with the 152nd of 450 kids on his lap.

"Lost in prayer?" The Reverend White smiled big and warm.

I must have been staring.

"No. No, I just ended up here. I didn't mean to," I stammered.

What did Naoki say?

Cross paths.

This wasn't going as I'd imagined. Not that I'd imagined busting up a Christian prayer meeting or whatever they called them. But whenever I'd imagined any kind of, like, run-in, like this, when I'd peeled the Reverend White's face off countless telephone poles, I'd never thought it would be this . . . cordial.

Still holding my hand, the Reverend White clasped his other hand around mine so he had me in a double shake, the intimate and intense shake of politicians and, apparently, preachers. "You know, young lady, this journey that I am going to lead you on, that we will be taking together, starting today, is righteous. We will save those who need to be saved. We will set on the Christian path those who have gone astray. And we will do this because we are good, God-fearing, AMERICAN Christians. And that's what you are, isn't it?"

"Um. No. Actually. That's really not me." I pulled back, though he didn't release my hand.

"Oh, not you?" The Reverend raised a white eyebrow.

I leaned back farther. Still in his grip. "No."

"It's perfectly all right to feel a little scared, my child," the Reverend said. "You—"

"I came. I came to return something to you," I said. And I wrenched my hand out of his grip, reached into my bag.

It was still there, the cross from my locker, its edges sharp against my fingers.

I'd kept it there all this time.

Foreshadowing?

*No*, I thought. *I just never clean out my bag. Maybe for good reason.*

I pulled the cross out, held it out in front of me.

The Reverend looked at the cross and then at me. "A gift?"

"I'm returning it," I said, turning the cross so Jesus was facing him.

The Reverend smiled weakly. "I'm sure I don't understand."

"Take it," I said, holding it up higher. "It's yours."

"Young lady." The Reverend put a delicate finger on the tip of the cross and lowered it.

"You know," I said, as conversationally as I could manage, "whoever glued this to my locker . . . It's not the first time.

Because I have two moms who are gay. Just because someone is queer doesn't mean you get to slap your . . . your stupid hate messages on a locker. My locker."

I held up the cross again, this time flat on my palm.

"This cross, this cross is a sign of God's love," the Reverend White said, delicately taking it from my hand. "Not a sign of hate." His voice was even deeper than before. "Homosexuality is a sin. Homosexuality undermines God's created order. As a servant of God, I am bound to hate the sin, but I am also bound to love the sinner."

"Well," I started. Words swirled like smoke in my mouth. I was afraid if I spoke, nothing would come out. "This stuff, pretty much everything you do so you can save us, it feels like hate, so you know." I could hear the tremor in my voice. "From here, it feels like hate."

I thought of the letters Tesla and I had gotten from my grandparents four years ago.

I opened mine first. I unfolded the letter typed on thick white paper that was taped inside a card with a picture of an angel on it.

"Wing women," Tesla called them.

I was reading it aloud, in the kitchen, because whenever I got a letter from my grandparents Mama Kate would always ask what it said. So I read it aloud.

"'Dear Montgomery,'" I said. My grandmother's notes were always written in pen on the card; it was my grandfather's messages that were typed and printed, trimmed to fit inside the cards exactly. "YOU HAVE A FATHER," I yelled because it was all in caps.

YOU HAVE A FATHER.

Mama Kate dropped the spoon she was holding. It clanged against the table. "Give it to me please, Monty."

It was October. On the table, there was a pumpkin we were supposed to carve. I was twelve and Tesla was seven. I scanned the letter fast, my eyes devouring each word. My grandfather had opened an investigation to find who the donor was, the person who donated the sperm that helped make Tesla and me. After months of searching, someone at the clinic told him the man was a Christian.

He is a good Christian.
It stills my heart to know this.

Mama Kate grabbed the letter.
*"Hey!"*
"Go find Momma Jo," she mumbled through her fingers. Her eyes scanned the letter. They were big like headlights.

I brought Momma Jo in the room, and they whispered. Then Momma Jo took us out for ice cream. Even though it was too cold. Tesla had too much whipped cream and got sick, and we came back early. That was when I found Mama Kate in the kitchen. On the phone. She told them she was not going to talk to them anymore.

Then she threw down the phone. And the battery came out of the case and skittered under the fridge. And the rest of the phone slid toward me, almost to my foot.

And I waited for Mama Kate to pick it up. Or look at me. Or say something.

Something like, "It's okay."

But instead she went to her room and cried.

I followed, feeling so scared it was as if being scared had hollowed me out to almost nothing. To a skin. I sat by the door. Momma Jo put Tesla to bed, then she came over and shooed me away, but I slipped back when she went inside.

I heard Mama Kate crying to Momma Jo.

"I can't," she said, her voice muffled.

"It's okay." Momma Jo's voice was so soft and sad. "I got you."

"I can't," Mama Kate cried.

All this might be the reason we don't really do Christmas so much, except that we go out for Chinese food and get presents.

All this might also be the reason I get a little tiny bit nervous whenever the phone rings at my house and Mama Kate answers it. Why I scan the mail when I get home, looking for my grandmother's handwriting. For that special pillowiness that comes with printed pages folded inside a card with a wing woman on the front.

*How fair is that?* I seethed, staring at the cross as the reverend placed it on an empty chair and stepped forward.

"If you are not here to pray and if you have not come for salvation, young lady, then I am afraid there is no place here for you." His eyes narrowed. His voice was so deep it could probably break up concrete.

"I'm not here to pray. I'm just here to tell you to leave us alone." My voice echoed off the walls around me. I stumbled back and bumped into a chair.

*An empty chair . . .*

I looked around.

*A room of empty chairs.*

That's when it hit me. It was after seven. The room was quiet because it was empty. The only person who'd bothered to come was Percy. But even Percy didn't stay.

"No one came," I breathed.

The Reverend cleared his throat. It was a yucky, phlegmy rumble. "I beg your pardon?"

But he heard me. I know he did, because he looked around.

"It's like a crappy birthday party in here," I whispered, turning around to take in the empty room. There was a sad little table in the corner of the room with sad little cans of soda and cookies in cellophane trays.

That no one would eat.

They were probably stale, I thought.

"I think you should leave," the Reverend said.

I tapped the top of the chair next to me, imagining Madison's nails clicking against the plastic. "Um, looks like there's no one to help you save the sinners of Aunty."

The Reverend clapped his hands soundlessly together. "I'm telling you to leave now. You are trespassing on private property and you must go immediately."

"Private property?" I pointed at the floor. "This is where people go for AA!"

"Young lady." His voice had gone from soup to squeaky. "I will be forced to call the police!"

The world melted away, and all I could see was him. His white suit with the yellowy cuffs. His thinning hair wagging as he shook his finger at me. A nervous giggle escaped my throat.

"You," he stuttered, "are a depraved soul. You will burn in hell with the rest of those who cannot or will not accept the love of Jesus Christ."

The Reverend White was just an angry old man who smelled like a baby's butt and had the power to put up a bunch of posters.

So what?

I guess it's easier to look big and important on a poster. Maybe that's why he liked them so much.

"I know," I said.

Which got me thinking about the difference between "I know" and "I see," which got me thinking about Naoki and Thomas and my moms, and how much I wanted to just be home.

*Screw this guy and his stupid "Save the Family,"* I thought.

The Reverend White was turning purple. "Get out!"

"Fine," I said, my voice echoing in the silence.

I turned stiffly and walked to the door, where I paused. I almost just said "goodbye." Like maybe out of habit.

*I should say something*, I thought, holding my hand against the cold steel of the door.

"So . . . screw you," I said. I wanted to say it like a punch, but it came out kind of lame. Like an impulse buy at the checkout.

As I pushed the door open, I heard him say, "Listen!" in this way that kind of caught in my gut.

I flung the door open and bolted down the street.

The next thing I heard . . .

*Clomp. Clomp.*

. . . was not something I think I could have predicted.

"Hey."

That voice. Deep. I looked up.

"Kenneth?"

# 12

FOR THE NEXT FOUR BLOCKS, WE PLAYED A WEIRD game of tag, where Kenneth kind of jogged beside me, then fell back. Then I stopped and waited. And he stopped and waited.

Then I walked really fast and he walked slowly but with strides long enough to keep pace with me.

Then I heard him say, "Dammit," and he just kind of strode up to me and pulled me over like a cop.

"Can I talk to you please?"

It would have been easier to say no if he hadn't asked nicely. Maybe I was just sick of fighting.

"Fine. We'll parkette." I pointed at a nearby city-groomed grassy knoll with two benches.

Kenneth nodded.

I walked to the first bench and dropped down into it. "What do you want?"

Kenneth stood for a bit, then sat down on the bench across from me. He kept looking at his boots. "First I'm just thinking," he said finally, still slowly, like a cowboy in a movie, "uh, that maybe you're some sort of crazy person."

"What makes you say that?"

"Can't think of a sane reason for you to pop in on a service like that," he said, running his hand over his short hair.

"It's a free country," I said.

Kenneth looked up. "I know it."

"Oh yeah?" I shot. "I'm sure you do. Let me tell you something about this *free* country. It doesn't mean you get to be a jerk and tell people their families are going to hell."

"Well"—Kenneth sat into the bench, like he was in a rocking chair on a porch in some Southern state—"technically, it does."

I stood up to leave or yell something. Who was this guy, anyway? Talking to me about freedom of speech?

Kenneth shook his head. "Hey. Sorry I said that. Just relax, okay? I'm sorry." He held up his hands, like someone showing he wasn't holding a weapon.

I dropped back down on the bench. "Uh, just so you know, so I'm not wasting your time, if you're trying to convert me, it's not going to happen."

"I don't think you need to be converted," Kenneth said. "Though it's strange you would show up at a place set for preaching when you don't want to be converted."

I thought about the empty chairs. It was like doing math with half an abacus. "Were you there?"

"I was waiting in the back for my ride home," he said, pulling a small paperback from his pocket and shaking it. "Reading."

"Reading. Really." I squinted at the book. *The Left Hand of Darkness* by Ursula K. Le Guin. *Huh.* "Science fiction?"

Kenneth shoved the book back in his pocket. "That's hard to believe?"

Every word fell with the weight of a chess piece between us.

"No. I just. Wait. So, if you don't care about converting and all that stuff, why did you . . ." My brain felt fuzzy, like I'd been time traveling all night and it was all Swiss cheese. "Why did you point me out to him at school?"

"My dad? I was pointing him to the *door*." Kenneth stamped hard on the ground, like he was trying to shake dust off his feet. "He promised me he wouldn't come by the school, and he broke his promise, as usual."

I bit my lip. "Oh. I just thought."

"I know what you thought." Kenneth frowned. "Look. I shouldn't have snapped at you. Even though you snapped at me. I just, with the 'preacher' thing. People have been calling me that since . . ." Kenneth waved the words away. "I say it a million times, and it doesn't matter, because no one listens. I am his son. Yes. But I'm not like him."

A car roared by.

"You don't believe in God? And Jesus? All of that?" I asked.

"A person can believe in God and Jesus Christ, can be a Christian, and not be like my father," he said.

"You don't want to be a good Christian?"

I could feel the cold of the night against the hot of my cheek.

"I don't know about that. I've met a lot of people calling themselves good Christians." He shook his head. "I'm not so sure about that." Kenneth looked up at the sky. Which I thought for a second was him praying.

*You look down when you pray?* I wondered.

I could see his breath a little against the night sky.

Then, with sudden momentum, like a kite string unraveling upward, he started speaking. "I want to talk to you about this, you know? And make you understand. Because. Because I know you see me and you think you know everything about me, but you don't. You see a preacher's son and you think that you know . . . But it's not like that. He does what he thinks he has to do, but I don't agree with it."

Kenneth popped out of his seat. "How about I don't like dropping into town after town and papering the place like we're getting ready for a garage sale?" he said, slapping his hand into his open palm. He started pacing, walking a circle around the bench. "How about I don't like calling stuff *sin* and saying people will go to *hell*? I don't think it's right. And I've studied the Bible my whole life just like he has. I don't see that the Bible says you have to do all this and break in on other peoples' lives and . . ."

Finishing his circle, Kenneth sank back into his bench. "I don't think that's what we're supposed to do. I don't think that's being a good Christian, to answer your question."

I could feel the bench cold pushing up against my butt.

Something about all this was making me feel like there was suddenly less oxygen in the world. Or too much.

Kenneth brushed his hand over his head again. "My father . . . There's so much he'll never see, and that's all there is to it. I just want . . . I just want to finish school and get out of here and go live my life somewhere."

Kenneth sighed.

*Wow*, I thought. *The statue speaks.*

"I'm just going on and on now," he said, sitting up and rubbing his thumb on his thigh.

"Yeah," I said. "I mean. Uh, thanks? I guess. I mean, I think . . . I know what you mean."

"I don't like talking much," he offered. "So I usually don't. Maybe none of that made any sense."

"I think it made sense," I said, crossing my arms to keep warm.

Kenneth leaned forward. "You okay?"

"Yeah, I'm fine."

Looking at him, still and for longer than I'd looked at the front of him up until now, I noticed Kenneth's face was freckled. Around his neck, I could see now, up close, a little coin with an eye on it.

"Nice eye," I said.

"Huh. It's, uh, for protection." Kenneth picked up the coin between his fingers and looked down at it. "Ordered it on the Internet," he added.

*What are the odds?*

Holding his hand out, Kenneth stammered, "Also. I. I just wanted to say. I didn't know, you know. I didn't know about your mothers. Even today. Until Naoki told me. Today. But just. She told me after we had our fight. To explain to me. A little of why you might be mad. I don't have any problem with that stuff. I just wanted you to know, that I didn't know until today and . . . I mean, it's fine by me."

"Oh." So Naoki was defending me? Maybe? For some stupid reason I suddenly wanted to cry.

"Thanks," I said. "I'm sorry. For yelling at you today."

How pointless is "I'm sorry" sometimes? I wasn't even 100 percent sure what I was sorry for. Or even if I was saying it to the right person.

"Forget it." Kenneth got off the bench. Took a step. "I should go. My ride is probably leaving soon."

"Um. Yeah. Me too. I mean, I should go." I stood. Took a step. Felt small under the night sky.

I looked at Kenneth standing there in the park. The new kid. In a weird, new little town.

"So," I said. "I'm not sure if Naoki told you, but, I have this, uh, we have this club . . ."

"Oh yeah." Kenneth looked at the ground.

"It's not like a regular school club," I said, shoving my hands in my pockets. "It's like a talk-about-cool-stuff . . . group. Like ESP, and ghosts, and sometimes if Thomas is in a mood we just talk about our horoscopes. You know. Like unexplained stuff. It's no big deal. I just thought maybe you could drop by."

Kenneth paused and looked down at his boots. "You guys talk about trepanation?"

"What's that?"

"You don't know?" Kenneth raised an eyebrow. "Should look it up."

"Oh yeah?"

My phone gave a weak buzz. It was nearly out of power. Fifteen percent. Enough for me to see twenty messages.

Twenty "Monty, where are you?" messages.

"Geez. I really gotta go," I said. Taking a step toward home, I turned. "This is going to sound dumb," I added, "but I'm glad we got to, you know, talk. Even if it's not something you like doing."

"Yeah." Kenneth's lips folded up into a small smile. "Well, maybe we'll do it again."

"Maybe," I said, turning and breaking into a run. "Bye."

# 13

WHEN I GOT HOME, THE KITCHEN WAS COURTROOM-
quiet except for a few electrical hums. Mama Kate and Momma
Jo stood on their respective sides of the kitchen island as I
walked in and slid onto a stool.

Momma Jo leaned forward on the island and clasped
her hands expectantly. "Please explain to your moms what
happened over the last four hours that meant you couldn't
respond to a single phone call or message. Even though
that is specifically why we got you a phone in the first
place."

"Whenever you're ready," Mama Kate added, pulling up a
stool.

Momma Jo raised a finger. "Wait. In this explanation, Montgomery, we will also expect some mention of what has happened recently that has made you so upset you had to slam the

door on your moms, who love you and do not deserve this treatment."

Mama Kate frowned. "Monty, we know something is wrong..."

"Okay." I took a breath. I placed my hands flat on the smooth surface of the marble island. "I didn't answer your texts, because I was at the Reverend White's 'Save the Family' thing."

"*What?*" Momma Jo screamed.

"Monty! Why would you go there?" Mama Kate gasped.

"Excellent question," Momma Jo noted. "Continue, Monty."

"I guess because... Okay." I shifted on my stool. Apparently there is no comfortable position when you're about to deliver this kind of speech. "So it all started... Wait."

After so many jumbled conversations that day, I had this thought that there was no way I could explain anything in any way that made sense.

I took another, even deeper breath.

"Okay. You know there was this whole Reverend White 'Save the Family' campaign thing."

Mama Kate looked at Momma Jo.

Momma Jo looked at me. "Go on."

"I mean, I go to a superignorant school where the only thing anyone gets is sports. You know? Fine. But then there's this campaign thing and it's just... it's like suddenly everything got more terrible. I don't know. I mean, Matt Truit was always an asshole..."

Momma Jo and Mama Kate exchanged confused stares.

"You don't know him, but he's a homophobic asshole, okay? I think even with recent events I can still say that that is true. Okay. And then there's Kenneth, and he's the Reverend White's son, and today after school Kenneth was standing there with his dad and I thought . . ." I took another breath. Like maybe a hyperventilating breath.

"You thought what?" Mama Kate touched my hand, like giving me a little push on the swing.

"I thought he was pointing me out to his dad. Because I have gay moms. But he wasn't. But I didn't know that. And I was mad. So I kind of yelled at him. Then I got in a fight with Naoki and Thomas, and Naoki yelled at me, and I walked away and I guess . . . I guess I just ended up outside the vigil place. And I just . . . I went in because I wanted to say 'Eff you,' I guess."

"Did you?" Momma Jo raised an eyebrow. "Say 'eff'?"

"Ummm." I replayed the exchange in my head. "Sort of. I think I said 'screw you.'"

"That could have been a pretty . . . intense experience," Mama Kate said.

Momma Jo whistled. "How *was* the vigil?"

I smiled. "There was no one there."

Momma Jo clapped her hands. "Ha! Well, there you have it! What do you know, Aunty? Not quite as homophobic as *some* people would think!"

"Yeah, I was kind of surprised. I guess it's been kind of a surprising day." Maybe *surprising* was the wrong word. Strange. No. Not strange.

"I didn't know this religious stuff was upsetting you so much." Mama Kate's voice was a wisp, it was so small. She looked down at her hands.

"It's not, like, just the religious stuff, really," I said, shifting my stare to the top of our kitchen island, which was covered in bills. "Sometimes I get tired of always feeling like I'm from Mars or something. I get that there's nothing wrong with who I am, okay?" I added, preempting the everyone-is-okay-including-kids-with-gay-moms talk. "I just wish more people got it. Like at school. Sometimes it feels like no one around here gets anything."

"Oh," Momma Jo scoffed, "it's not an around-here thing, Monty. Anywhere you go there are going to be some clueless and stupid people. Get used to it."

"Great," I mumbled.

Mama Kate gave Momma Jo a look of psychic mom intensity.

"Okay. Mama Kate would want me to say, not everyone is clueless and stupid." Momma Jo softened. "People. People who live in Aunty, who live in big cities, who grow up religious or gay or what-have-you. People are complicated. Sometimes it's more than just 'they don't get it.' Sometimes there's more to people than you can see."

Now you tell me.

The doorbell rang. Momma Jo pushed off the island and jogged to the front door, calling over her shoulder, "Don't move!"

Mama Kate was quiet. Aside from the creak of Momma Jo's

footsteps, and the muffled sound of her opening the door, the whole kitchen fell under some crazy spell of silence. Even the fridge was uncharacteristically chill, not humming or shaking or doing that weird ticking thing it's started to do after I slammed the door too hard with my foot because my arms were full of snacks. Staring at Mama Kate, I could feel every breath like a tidal wave.

"I didn't want to tell you about the Reverend White stuff," I said, finally, "because I know, with your dad . . . I know talking about that stuff upsets you. And it really—it's *not* a big deal."

"Monty." Mama Kate smiled a sad smile. "Just because something makes me sad or upsets me doesn't mean it's a terrible thing I can't talk about. It's okay to be sad."

"Okay," I said, sitting up. "Sure. Right."

*How is it okay to be sad?* I thought. *It's the worst to be sad.*

My face must have looked all twisted or something. Mama Kate curled her hand over her lip. "You don't think it's okay to be sad?"

"Oh yeah, I mean, it's *fine*." I kicked the island softly.

*Thump. Thump. Thump.*

"What are you afraid is going to happen if someone is sad?" Mama Kate asked quietly.

*Thump. Thump. Thump.*

In the hallway I could hear Momma Jo hunting for her wallet and cursing.

My toes were ringing.

*They could leave,* I thought. *They could fold in on themselves and just disappear. They could not come out of the bedroom, ever.*

"Crappy things," I said, finally.

"Well," Mama Kate said, "I'm sure having someone be sad is pretty scary."

I swallowed hard. "Right."

Like the edge of a cliff. A dream you can't wake up from.

"I know," Mama Kate said, "it scares me when I see you upset."

"Aha! But it's okay to be sad and upset," I sniffed, pointing playfully, as I blinked through my suddenly sweaty eyes. "Right?"

"Right," Mama Kate said. "So, maybe . . . maybe it wouldn't be the worst thing if we were sad sometimes. Maybe it's not the end of the world. Because we have each other."

I watched her hand reach over and grab mine.

Mama Kate has the best hands. Maybe that was weird to think. But, really, they're never clammy and they never grab too hard. Imagine having a mom with a bony, sweaty hand.

That would be terrible.

I could taste the tears on my lips. "I know it's stupid, I'm just, sometimes I'm scared if it all gets too bad . . . I'll lose everyone."

"Oh, Monty"—Mama Kate's face was all rivers—"you won't."

Then we basically just . . . cried for a bit. I don't know how long. Then I wiped my nose on an oven mitt, which is gross, but I couldn't find a paper towel, or a tablecloth.

Momma Jo tiptoed in and slid a box of what smelled like cheese-and-pepperoni heaven on the counter.

"We ordered before you came back from your *vigil*," Momma

Jo said, walking over to kiss the top of my head. "I don't know if they serve snacks at vigils these days."

"They have cookies," I said. "But I didn't eat any."

"Good girl." Momma Jo looked down at the box, then up at me and Mama Kate. I guess we were both sniffing a bit. "Soooo . . . we've had a good talk. I figure we can take a break and say we will continue this conversation on a future date. Yes?"

"Sure." I went to pop off the counter to grab a plate, but Mama Kate had me in a bear hug.

Then Momma Jo had me in a bear hug.

Then Tesla came downstairs in her workout outfit, likely lured by the smell of cheese, and I guess then we had a really long, kind-of-cheesy family bear hug.

And then I had probably the best pizza I've had in forever.

\* \* \*

Five slices later, I went upstairs to go online, to find Thomas and tell him what the heck was going on, and I sat down on the bed and there it was.

The cross.

The cross!

*What?*

I was just about to lose my crap when I looked up and Tesla was standing in the doorway.

"You can have it," she said. "I didn't mean to hurt your feelings."

"You didn't," I said.

"Yes I did," Tesla said quietly.

She had these jammies on. We have matching ones. From Christmas. Pink for her and blue for me. With the feet and the trap door in the back. She normally never wore them.

I wondered how much Tesla could hear me talking with the moms downstairs. Maybe it was just as scary for her, having a sister freaking out.

Tesla ran her toe in an arc over the floor. When she's sad, my sister looks like me. When she looks sad and when she's not jogging, our shared genes shine through.

"You can have a cross," I said, feeling like more of a jerk than one would ever imagine possible. "You can do whatever you want. I mean, who am I to say . . ."

"I don't want to be a Christian," Tesla said, leaning into the doorway. "I just wanted to see what it was like. Like an experiment. Because other people do it and because I didn't know what it would be like to talk to God."

"What was it like?"

"It was okay, I guess." Tesla scanned the debris of my room. No doubt wondering whether she would eventually discover her don't-have-to-clean-to-be-cool gene.

"Well," I sighed, "as long as no one was hurt."

*You're one up on me*, I added silently to myself.

"Yeah," Tesla mumbled, her chin to her chest, "I did use it to pray to win against the Gophers."

I picked up the cross. This one had smooth edges. The same mashed-up face, though.

I looked over at Tesla.

213

*Geez, I didn't even know she had another big game. Was it a play-off?*

"How'd it go? I mean, did you win?"

Tesla frowned. "We lost," she said, sinking to the ground.

"Sorry," I said, lowering myself across from her.

Tesla started lightly pounding the floor in front of her with her fist, like she was flattening a pancake. "It was stupid. You have to train to win, not pray. Anyway, we'll win next year."

It was like I was standing on the business end of a batting range with no bat. Just lots. And lots. Of balls.

Flaming balls of *You were wrong, Montgomery.*

*Nice one, Montgomery.*

*Way to misread everyone and everything, Montgomery.*

*Way to go.*

*Oh and did I mention you're an amazing sister? That's right because you're not.*

Apparently you can be someone who spends a lifetime on the Internet looking up stuff and still not know crap about the world around you.

"Okay, well," Tesla said, scrambling to her feet. "See you tomorrow."

"Hey," I said. "Do you want the cross? I mean, you can have it. Even if you don't want to pray to win. It's cool."

"No," Tesla said, shaking her head.

"Okay, well"—I stood and walked over to my desk—"I'll put it in a drawer for you. In case you want it for later."

"Or in case *you* want it for later," Tesla said.

"Right."

I listened to her little foot pads as she walked back to her room and shut the door.

Then I opened the drawer again and looked at the cross. I took the Eye off my neck and shut it in the same drawer.

# 14

☺ Time travel

I WONDER ALL THE TIME IF I WERE TO MEET A version of myself in the future or the past whether I would want to talk to myself. It would be tempting to tell past-me all this stuff I know now, but then again I would probably screw up the time continuum by saying anything. Maybe I could just say something really simple, like "Relax, it's not that bad."

I don't know if I would believe me. It would probably depend on the timing.

After my "vigil adventure," as Momma Jo called it, instead of having Pizza Night, the Sole family started To-Be-Continued Night, where we talk about what's going on at school, still over pizza. Sometimes this devolves into this general Q and A, where my moms just ask me a million questions, but sometimes it's nice to just talk about what's going on in our lives.

Once in a while, instead of grilling Tesla and me, Mama Kate and Momma Jo tell us about stuff that they're finding hard.

Which is kind of interesting.

Momma Jo misses playing sports, but she doesn't like the women who run the sports teams in Aunty. She says they are all wimps.

Also, some of the people on Tesla's soccer team are jerks. Like this one girl Tammy, who told everyone that Tesla was a boy's name.

"Um," Momma Jo said, "it's a super*cool* name of a supercool scientist-inventor, so they can just be quiet."

"Just tell them it's the name of a fairy," I said.

"Good idea," Tesla noted.

*　*　*

I'm not sure if talking about school makes it suck less, or if seeing the Reverend White's failed rally for hating homosexuals inspired a little optimism in me.

I did wonder about Percy for a while after I saw him running out of the building that night. Thomas heard from someone in his English class that he'd been paid by the Reverend White to put up the crosses at school. *Hey, cashmere ain't cheap, darling*, as Thomas would say.

I thought of saying something to him, but then the next time I ran into Percy in the halls, I realized I kind of didn't care.

It's just a cross.

I've basically quit Yoggy cold turkey since Tiffany headed back to Michigan. I did try, for a while, to keep my Yoggy habit going, but it's just not the same without her there.

I hope she's happier now. I also, greedily, am hoping she's somewhere continuing her research. Though she's probably not.

The girl who works at Yoggy now is obsessed with carbohydrates. Now *all* the fro-yo is carb-free.

Which to me is hilarious because it's like, is it *really* carb-free or is it carb-free based on Tiffany's labeling system?

Who knows?

Either way, the new girl is, like, a size two blonde who wears flip-flops and has, like, a zillion tan lines. I'm pretty sure she wouldn't give me any free toppings.

In other news, it turns out Matt Truit has some sort of major heart condition. I overheard Madison Marlow telling the Parte twins that it's a genetic thing. They found it when they were doing tests on him in the hospital.

Madison said her mom said it was because Matt's parents were originally from Los Angeles.

Apparently, according to Madison's mom, people from Los Angeles are prone to heart conditions. Because they all do drugs.

Now Matt can't play basketball or football. He did end up in the play, last minute. I guess they got Coach Choreographer to figure out some less stressful fighting moves for him.

Probably some light slaps.

One day we were walking down the hall and Thomas was wearing this big pink daisy lapel pin, and I saw Matt point it out, but then he just didn't say anything else.

And I didn't say anything, either.

* * *

After my Reverend White run-in, the Mystery Club took a brief hiatus.

Partly because Thomas was up to his well-sculptured eyebrows in production stuff for *The Outsiders* and partly because I was feeling a little burnt out.

After all that had happened, I kind of wanted everything to feel normal and not so mysterious for a bit. For two weeks I didn't even look up mystery stuff on the Internet. I just watched reality TV and cooking shows, with a possible goal of trying to figure out how to make my own gelato.

Sometime around the end of November, Naoki suggested we start up again and invite Kenneth to a meeting. She wanted to try table-tipping. Naoki looked it up and apparently it's supposed to work better with four people.

Naoki: OK? Cuz if you're not comfortable. We don't have to. Totally no big deal.
Me: It's cool. Let's do it.

Table-tipping turned out to be kind of a flop, but it was fun to try. Thomas pointed out that we were more "desk-tipping" than table-tipping. Kenneth added that it was possible

Mrs. Dawson's desk was too heavy to tip. Naoki thought maybe Mrs. Dawson's snow globe collection, which we were afraid to take off the desk, was throwing us off balance. I noticed you could throw the whole thing by just moving the table with your knees. We gave it a 1.5.

A week later, I called a special meeting to discuss the Eye. Core members only.

"Not because of anything against Kenneth," I explained as we all filed into Mrs. Dawson's classroom that afternoon.

"I kind of owe you guys, I think. I mean, I didn't talk about the Eye with you when everything was happening, even though I said I would. So it's kind of a makeup session," I said, sitting on a desk, placing the Eye next to me.

Naoki was mostly interested in the incantation. She called it a crazy cosmic haiku (although the syllables didn't match up). At the opening of the meeting, she wrote it out on the chalkboard.

In sight
not see
black light
not be

"'In *sight*,'" Naoki whispered, "'not *see*.' Like a riddle. What is in sight but not seen?"

"What did you actually see with the Eye on?" Thomas asked.

"People I hated." I shrugged.

"And you would see it and . . . what?" Naoki looked at the Eye catching sunlight on the desk. It looked kind of menacing now.

"Something would happen to them. Something bad. The girl at the soccer game disappeared, you know, over the edge of the stands. Matt stopped talking."

"Didn't he have a heart attack?" Naoki asked. "It's, like, stopping."

"Doesn't sound like you really saw anything other than what you already knew," Thomas said.

"Your point?"

Grabbing a piece of chalk, Thomas grinned. "Really," he said, sketching out the text on the whiteboard, "what you've purchased is Eye of What You Already Know."

"The Eye of Assumption," Naoki chimed in. "The Eye of Preconception."

"Or we could say that the Eye really wasn't so much an eye, because I didn't see anything with it," I said.

"Well"—Thomas's grin grew so big it hit the sides of his face—"that's what you get for $3.99."

"Wow," I gasped in mock amazement, "how long have you been waiting with that one?"

"At least an hour." Thomas patted himself on the back.

"It was $5.99," I said.

"Fine." Thomas stuck out his tongue.

"You're both so silly," Naoki sighed happily.

I slumped. "I mean, maybe this makes me sound like a jerk,

but I have to say, it was . . . nice. It's like, I expected so many of the people at this school to be crappy. And with the Eye, it felt like I could do something about it. But I guess that's not really *knowing*, you know, per se."

"Not really," Naoki agreed.

"So once you know you may or may not have a loaded weapon at your disposal, what do you do?"

"You should throw it off a cliff," Thomas said.

"Someone could find it and pick it up," I pointed out.

"Well, they won't know the incantation thing, right?"

After extensive haggling, Naoki remembered that the original ad had a different stone in it.

"You said it was clear, right? Or white? So maybe this *isn't* the Eye of Know," she said. "Maybe it's something else. You should return it and get the real one."

"Buyer beware," Thomas tutted.

"Well, the other option is we just hide it," Naoki added. "At least this way you don't have to worry about someone else finding it."

After the meeting, Naoki gave me a little hug.

Naoki said she thinks the Eye is just another part of my Internet searching. It's not the end; it's just another one of the many mysteries out there. It's a lesson, she said, part of my overall quest for knowledge.

"It's like what T. S. Eliot said about exploring." Naoki stretched her hands high above her head and closed her eyes. "At the end of it, what you know is you."

"That sounds awesome," I said.

So I wrapped up the Eye and sent it back to Manchester. Fortunately I still had the address on the packaging under my bed. Because I had had the foresight not to clean my room. Point for me.

I added a note that said I thought I had the wrong Eye and would love to get an actual Eye of Know if they had one. I hope maybe someday they'll send me one. Until then I'll just keep looking.

☺ Me.

For my birthday a week later, my moms got me a new laptop and driving lessons. For more, faster web surfing and for possible future exploration outside the Internet.

I also got a hundred dollars to buy new clothes. Which I'm thinking is possibly a good idea.

I mean, Momma Jo's clothes are comfy, but there are other clothes out there.

Maybe even new clothes.

Tesla, who is now MVP of her soccer team, gave me this picture she took of me and her from a year earlier, at this picnic or something.

If you look close, we're like jumbled puzzles made up of the same pieces. Something in our eyes and noses. Our messy habits. Our crooked smiles. I never noticed how our smiles are alike before.

I told Mama Kate, and she laughed, then said, "You should smile more. I love your smile."

"It's my smile," Momma Jo said.

I smiled extra big. "Nice!"

The first thing I opened on my brand-new laptop was an e-mail from Kenneth with a link to the craziest thing I have ever seen on the Internet, a site about people who actually drill holes into the tops of their skulls to increase brain blood flow. To improve psychic powers. That's what trepanation is!

Me: Dude. I can't believe there is a video of someone drilling a hole in her head on the Internet.
Kenneth: Look up speaking in tongues. Great videos.
Me: Ok. You look up "levitation" and "dog."
Kenneth: Good idea.

For the night of my birthday, Thomas's dad lent him the car, and Naoki and Thomas and I went out to this part of the desert off the highway that's right by this great big canyon. We got there just as the sun was setting in this way it does in the desert, with a million weird and crazy colors. You would never find them in a "sunset" palette at the Home Depot.

And we got out of the car.

And we watched the sunset, feeling good the way you do in California when everything is so beautiful.

"This is officially the coolest thing to happen on my birthday," I said.

We all stood on the edge of the horizon, like the end of the world before it dips down into vastness, and we put our hands in the air and breathed in.

And my eyes got wide, and I tried to just take in all the world in front of me in that moment.

I looked at the sky and let my brain go soft like a sponge.

I tried to absorb all that is the big, strange universe, and all the strange mysteries in it.

Including me. Mystery me.

"Pretty amazing, huh?" Naoki mused, her hands stretched open, her eyes closed.

"Yeah," I said. "I know."

# Acknowledgments

This novel would not exist if it were not for the many people who have supported me through this and other lofty endeavors.

Thank you to Sam Hiyate and Ali McDonald at The Rights Factory.

Thank you to the magical Charlotte Sheedy. Thank you to my incredible editors Connie Hsu at Roaring Brook and Lynne Missen at Penguin Canada. And to copy editor Christine Ma. Thank you to the incredible Eleanor Davis, Katherine Guillen, and Andrew Arnold for the gorgeous cover. And to all my writer friends for their support and advice, with special thanks to Daniel Heath Justice.

Thank you to all my queer families, work and play. Thank you to all the queer parents out there, who are fighting the good fight, loving the good love, every day.

The concept of the Mystery Club was sparked on a porch during a meeting with Toronto's one and only Science Club, which has marked so many. Thank you to all its members: Suzanne, Christine, Ali, Sorrell, Carolyn, and Lindy.

The voice of Monty first appeared on a bus in Portland, Oregon, on a trip I took with Heather Gold, who has my heart and has given me more support than I could have ever imagined possible.

Finally, thank you to my parents, who banked and inspired this book of spells.

# Don't miss THIS ONE SUMMER

written by Mariko Tamaki and illustrated by Jillian Tamaki

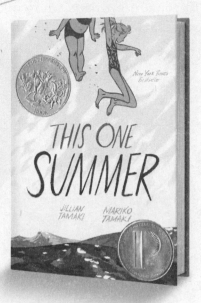

A *NEW YORK TIMES* BESTSELLER

A CALDECOTT HONOR BOOK

A MICHAEL L. PRINTZ HONOR BOOK

★ "A triumph." —*KIRKUS REVIEWS*, starred review

★ "Wistful, touching, and perfectly bittersweet." —*BOOKLIST*, starred review

★ "Poignant and melancholy." —*THE BULLETIN*, starred review

★ "This captivating graphic novel presents a fully realized picture of a particular time in a young girl's life, an in-between summer filled with yearning and a sense of ephemerality." —*SCHOOL LIBRARY JOURNAL*, starred review

First Second